The Remarkable Mrs. Peel

Emma hit the robot like a missile, knocking it off balance and down. Landing lightly on her feet, Emma grabbed for the fallen branch again and slammed it down like a spear through the "head" of the creature. It entered the broken gap and continued through. Components smashed, and a stench of burning plastic hit Emma's nostrils. Sparks danced across the robot's face. Emma twisted the stick and heard further damage. . . .

"Well done, Mrs. Peel!" Steed called.

THE

AVENGERS

JOHN PEEL AND DAVID ROGERS

Too Many Targets

A TOM DOHERTY ASSOCIATES BOOK
NEW YORK

THE AVENGERS: TOO MANY TARGETS

A Tor Book
Published by Tom Doherty Associates, Inc.
175 Fifth Avenue
New York, NY 10010

Tor Books on the World Wide Web:
http://www.tor.com

ISBN: 0-812-58909-2
Library of Congress Card Catalog Number: 90-36129

First edition: November 1990
First mass market edition: June 1998

Printed in the United States of America

0 9 8 7 6 5 4 3 2 1

FOREWORD

A new novel about the Avengers? *All* of the Avengers—Steed, Mrs. Gale, Mrs. Peel, Tara King, *and* Dr. Keel. Well, I never!

It must be some twenty-eight years since I first wrote an Avengers novel with Peter Leslie—and still it goes on. Good luck to both of you. Onward and upward.

All success for a bestseller. At this rate, we can look forward to the Avengers seeing us into the twenty-first century.

Patrick Macnee

THE AVENGERS

Too Many Targets

1 STRANGEST IN THE NIGHT

It had stopped raining, finally, but clouds still covered the moon. The tracker paused and bent to examine the muddy ground. The three other hunters moved quietly to join him, their spears held at the ready, their shields high. The men wore nothing on their muscular, dark-skinned bodies but loincloths and armbands of knotted grasses. Around their foreheads were bands of colorful cloth.

The tracker gestured. On the border of the coppice was a smudged but unmistakable footprint. "Gorilla," he grunted, somewhat unnecessarily. That was, after all, what they were hunting. "Close, by the look of it."

The leader of the band—a tall, surly brute of a man with a wiry red beard—nodded. With a gesture of his spear, he sent two men to the left and joined the third man on the right. Splitting up, each about ten feet from his neighbor, they moved off silently into the fringe of trees. Each of them was scanning the bushes and listening for the slightest sound that would betray the location of their quarry.

For a few moments, nothing stirred. Like a line of ghosts, they passed through the undergrowth. Then, with an earsplitting roar, a huge, shaggy body threw itself from the shadows. Two heavy, muscular arms snaked out to grab one of the hunters. The man screamed, struggling to raise his spear. Too late. Snarling, showing its huge, yellowed fangs, the beast pressed the captive man with its arms. The man gasped, then went deadly silent. His companions watched in awestruck bewilderment as his body was tossed aside like a feather.

Their reactions slowed by the encounter, the other hunters paused. Then, shaking off their terror, they closed in on the anthropoid, spears raised. Cornered, the gorilla growled. Raising his arms in one fluid movement, the bearded leader threw his spear at the creature.

The weapon struck it high on the chest. The spear snapped with a dull thud; the beast didn't even flinch. The broken shaft fell at the gorilla's huge feet.

The men stared in total disbelief at the anthropoid as it beat its chest with its massive fists and issued a deep-throated growl. Two of the hunters drew back, seeking the safety of the trees. Screaming for his companions to follow him, the leader of the surviving trio snatched up the spear dropped by his slain companion and heaved the weapon squarely at the gorilla's hairy form. The spear rattled off the beast's right shoulder, vanishing into the gloom. The enraged creature snatched a second spear out of the air, shredding the weapon into matchwood with its mighty fists. Screaming again, the gorilla lunged at the men.

Horrified at the sight, the men turned and ran. Recognizing that its foes were routed, the anthropoid stopped dead in its tracks and watched the vague shadows disappear. Roaring out its grim pleasure to the still night air, it dropped back to a crouch, its knuckles on the ground. With a rolling gait, it ambled past the lifeless body of the downed hunter and disappeared with a grunt into the darkness of the trees.

Their spirits broken, the three men fled for their lives until they reached the safety of their cars, parked beneath a sign that read—LONDON—27 MILES.

The red-bearded man flung open his car door, peering breathlessly back over his shoulder. Nothing stirred. He threw his shield and perspiration-soaked headband into the back of the Vauxhall, then scrambled hastily into his trousers, shirt, socks, and shoes. Without so much as a glance at his companions, he jumped into his car and gunned it down the road—back toward his home in Chelmsford.

It had stopped raining, finally. The streets were dark, and large puddles of water covered the pavement. The streetlights were uncommonly subdued, their circles of light smaller and softer than normal. Nothing stirred on the roads, and the houses and shops were closed tight against the cold night air.

Keller leaned against a lamp post, catching his breath, panting. The nagging stitch in his side was getting worse, but he did not dare to stop and rest. He had to warn the Department. Pushing the wet hair out of his eyes, he looked back over his shoulder. His pursuer was nowhere to be seen. Dragging his mackintosh closer about him to cut off the evening chill, Keller started to run again. He splashed through the puddles, careless of the soaking his trouser bottoms were getting.

It was no use; the pain in his side was unbearable—he couldn't go much farther now. His eyes burned with the yellow flashes that accompanied the sharp, searing bouts of pain. He knew that he would shortly collapse. But the Department had to be warned—*it had to be!*

Staggering toward another welcome lamp post, he placed his shoulder against it and took his bearings. The streets all looked the same to him. He didn't know this neighborhood, or its maze of back alleys dating back to the end of the War. Nor could his tired eyes read the street signs. What he could make out, though, in a puddle of light, was the familiar red of a telephone box.

Dragging together his weary limbs, he staggered on, clawing for the kiosk door. He prayed silently that the box hadn't been vandalized. Clutching the handle, he flung the door open and collapsed into the dry interior. With a wave of relief, he saw that the phone was intact.

Keller dug into his trouser pocket for a handful of change. Coins spilled onto the floor, but he didn't bother to retrieve them. Selecting a half-crown and several sixpences, he dumped them on the top of the phone books. He had made up his mind whom to call. Lifting the telephone receiver to his ear, he began to dial the number he had committed to memory.

The phone burred in his ear. Rubbing the condensation off the square of glass directly opposite his nose, he looked back down the street. His heart almost stopped. Was that a figure moving, down at the end of the road? He found it difficult to focus his weary eyes. In a panic, he muttered, "Come on! Come on!"

On the tenth ring, the phone was abruptly answered. "Yes?" snapped a curt, suspicious voice.

"Charles," he gasped thankfully. "Charles, it's Keller."

"I don't know anyone by that name. How did you get this number?"

Keller realized he should have known that—Charles had retired a year before he had joined the Department. "Steed," he gasped. "Code 17–20, Alpha Priority." He hoped that this had been the signal back then also.

"My God!" Charles answered, all anger and doubt drained from his voice. "Where are you, man?"

"I'm not sure." Keller glanced outside again. The shadows were still once more. "On the run. Listen, urgent: we've got trouble."

"What sort of trouble?"

"Double agent . . ." Taking a deep breath and fighting back the terrible agony in his side, Keller continued. "The worst possible kind . . . someone you wouldn't suspect . . . I—I made contact and—"

He broke off as a shadow fell over him from outside the kiosk. Spinning around, he had just enough time to scream before the glass in front of his eyes shattered. The telephone receiver slipped from his fingers as he raised his hands in an attempt to block the next blow. It was a defensive reflex that failed utterly. A fist whiplashed its way through the shards of broken glass and a heavy blow struck him sharply behind the ear.

Lights flashed before his eyes and Keller collapsed, dead, his limp head crashing into the door of the telephone box.

Above his head, the phone spun crazily on the end of its cord. Charles's voice could be heard, tinnily: "Keller? Keller? Are you there?"

A hand reached out, drew up the receiver and placed it to a face. "I'm sorry," the killer said, "but your caller has been disconnected." Fastidiously replacing the receiver in its cradle—and with a last look at Keller's crumpled body, which now lay half in and half out of the shattered telephone-box door—the killer moved off, humming cheerfully to himself.

The station clock showed that it was now half-past three in the morning. The platform was deserted. Although it was a busy commuter stop in the day, when office workers poured into the city, Ridgely Halt was absent of movement. The stationmaster had locked the gates at eleven sharp and then cycled home to his waiting bed. Nothing had stirred at the station since then.

As the clock's hand pulsed forward, moving on to the next minute, a pair of hands appeared at the edge of the platform. Gripping the white-painted edge, their owner managed to lever himself onto the terrace. For a scant moment he lay there, panting. Then he forced his tired arms to push down and managed to stagger to his feet.

Slowly he dragged his way down the platform. Harrison's appearance had once been impeccable; he usually dressed in a sharp, dark-striped businessman's suit with a crisp white carnation in his lapel. The flower was now browned and faded, hanging on by its withering stem. His clothes were in a dreadful state. His expensive Italian shoes were scuffed and torn, and then plastered with mud. His Savile Row suit was shredded in several places from thorns, and trickles of blood from his exposed skin had stained the fabric. His hat was long since lost, and his tie was a mess.

Harrison reached the gate that led out into the darkened streets, clawing at it feebly. Locked! Lacking the strength to haul himself over the barrier, he looked about wildly, seeking inspiration.

Under a small lamp positioned outside the ticket office, he saw the telephone. Pushing his tired body away from the locked gate, he stumbled to the telephone box. It took him two attempts to drag the receiver from its cradle, his numb fingers refusing to obey his will. Pawing through his pockets, he dragged out several coins. Damn it, he thought to himself as he attempted to ease the coins into the pay slots. After several attempts, he managed it and dialed a number.

It was answered on the first ring, and he sighed.

"Harrison here," he managed to get his aching jaw to say. "Patch me through to Mother."

There was a brief pause, and then the sharp, measured accent that he recognized too well. "Mother."

"Listen carefully," Harrison gasped. "Not much time. I was right—there is a double agent."

"Are you sure, Harrison?" Mother sounded worried, as well he might. Since that Philby affair, British Intelligence could no longer be certain of anything, it seemed.

"Almost had me," Harrison answered, fighting for every word. "Managed to get away. I'm at Ridgely Station. Don't have long, he is—" Hearing a noise behind him, he turned, and then screamed.

His attacker was on him in an instant. It took one blow—one deadly whipcracklike punch. The attacker then tossed Harrison's body aside like a sack of old clothes. The phone swung free; Mother's shock at what he had heard registered shrilly from the earpiece. Catching the receiver in mid-swing, Harrison's attacker placed it to his face and said in a clear, precise voice: "I'm sorry, but your caller has been cut off." Placing the receiver neatly back onto its cradle, the killer bent down and grabbed the collar of Harrison's suit. He heaved the lifeless bundle to its feet and set the dead man onto the railway bench positioned outside the station's booking office, where it would surely be found the following morning. Looking with displeasure at the faded carnation in Harrison's lapel, he shook his head and snatched the flower away. He dropped it into the nearest litter bin. He then took the fresh red carnation from his own lapel and slid it neatly into the dead man's buttonhole. Nodding in satisfaction, he tilted his bowler to a rakish angle and ambled off into the night, swinging his umbrella in cheery abandon.

2 Mixed Doubles . . . as in Agents

John Steed believed in living a life as close to perfection as humanly possible. He had spent most of his adult years determining what that meant as far as his own tastes went, and then proceeded to surround himself with possessions that pleased his eye, his ear, or his palate. This had left his flat decorated in a variety of conflicting styles, but it never ceased to bring him satisfaction. Some people thought, for example, that the upended tuba filled with fresh flowers was perhaps a trifle too avant-garde for an English gentleman, but no one would dare say it to his face. His well-known impeccable manners and attire labeled him firmly as belonging to that vanishing breed of eccentrics, and if he chose to own a flower-filled tuba—well, then, there must be something inherently British about it.

To accompany his rather off-beat decor, Steed had evolved a near-perfect lifestyle. Unless he was on a case, he rose at eleven in the morning and then took a leisurely bath and shave. He seldom ate breakfast, but if there was a busy day ahead of him, he might take a light snack with his noontime pot of Earl Grey. He inevitably accompanied the pot by reading the *Guardian*—perhaps less traditional than the *London Times*, but he preferred the reporting style.

His afternoons would then be spent in the pursuit of either culture or young ladies—or, preferably, cultured young ladies. The evenings—well, that depended on his social calendar and the young ladies already mentioned. He rarely retired to bed before one in the morning, and frequently much later. All in all, a comfortable and enjoyable existence.

On the other hand, without the benefit of his work, such a lifestyle could rapidly bore one to death—particularly a man such as Steed, who was used to courting danger. Though Steed worked somewhat irregularly, when he did work, he put his heart into it and enjoyed his profession—although he regularly risked grave injury to life and limb in the process.

It was his work that made all things enjoyable for Steed and broke the otherwise routine pattern of his life.

This morning was just like any other. Having emptied his teacup and ritually poured himself a second, he began to scan the morning paper for any item of news to interest one of Her Majesty's Whitehall minions—the shadowy faces who risk all to keep Britain's shores free of subversion, the men and women who lay their lives on the line to protect Britannia's flame. For a second his eyes paused on a short filler about a killer gorilla supposedly on the loose in Surrey. That sounded as if it might be . . . no. Such was impossible. With a sigh, he read that the local Chief Constable believed that the story was just a wild rumor and that the person responsible for breaking the back of a building-site worker was an escaped convict the police were searching for. Mentally wishing the police well in their search, Steed continued to scan the paper.

The telephone bell invaded his reverie. Steed scooped it up on the third ring. The caller's voice was unfamiliar for a second, and then Steed stiffened in anticipation.

"Steed? Trouble."

A broad grin broke Steed's handsome features. It was partially caused by the thought of impending action, and partly out of recognition of the voice—a voice he hadn't heard in many a long year. "Charles! My dear fellow, how are you?"

"No time for the niceties, Steed," growled the voice. "Do you remember Dawson Street? Meet me there as soon as possible." Without waiting for Steed's reply, Charles broke the line.

Of course Steed remembered. Agents never forget a "safe" house, and Steed was the best in the field. Everyone said so.

Smiling as he replaced the receiver, Steed shrugged his pearl-gray jacket over his waistcoat, took a last sip of tea, and then headed for the door. From the rack there, he selected a matching bowler, which he carefully set on his thick, dark hair, and then an umbrella. Taking a last glance into the full-length mirror, checking the elegant styling of the Savile Row suit, the angle of the bowler, and the shine on his shoes, he hurried down the stairs and out to the garage at the rear of his flat.

The Bentley stood ready and waiting to be off. Steed was immensely proud of his newly acquired 1933 model—here was a car! Not like the boxes on wheels that they made these days. Minis! Fords! Jaguars! Ha! None of them could hold a candle to the stark beauty standing peerlessly before him. Vaulting over the Bentley's door, he slid into the driver's seat and gunned the engine. The car started with a pleasing purr. Letting out the brake, he drove out of the yard, spun the steering wheel and, with a gentle touch of the accelerator, turned into the London traffic.

Enjoying the envious looks of other motorists as he sped along, Steed could not shake off the uneasy feeling that something big was afoot. Why had Charles telephoned him? Why not Mother? Nevertheless, it would be good to see Charles again. It had been three—no, closer to four—years now since he had seen his old boss. Charles had held most of British Intelligence in working order for almost fifteen years, until he was finally ordered to retire back in 1964. Many hundreds of successful operations had begun and ended with reports on Charles's desk. In fact, Steed owed his present job to the foresight and patronage that Charles had extended.

Though he worked ostensibly for the Intelligence arm of the British government, Steed was neither spy nor counterspy. A free spirit in many ways, he was assigned to work on cases considered too sensitive, too difficult, or simply too bizarre for other operatives to tackle. Somehow or other, it was the third type that he seemed to be handed the most frequently—and that he most enjoyed. Steed had passed an apprenticeship in conventional espionage, but had found the work depressingly boring, underpaid, and pointless. This position he held now was fascinating, well salaried, and better suited to his tastes. The job often left him saving—well, perhaps not the world (he gladly left that to other operatives, the real-life counterparts of that fictional fellow with the double-O prefix), but certainly extensive portions of the British Empire and/or the inhabitants thereof. It was rewarding in all aspects.

Another of the enjoyable points about his position was that he was allowed to select his own assistants. In the past, these had been mostly amateurs in the espionage game, chosen by Steed for their expertise in other fields of work. The first of these had been David Keel, a medical doctor whose fiancée had been shot down in a London street by a drug gang that Steed was after. Keel had helped Steed in their capture, and the two men had somehow gravitated together. Despite this, they had frequently disagreed and the relationship had been somewhat stormy, with Steed's ruthlessness in getting his own way being mostly to blame. Steed nevertheless harbored good memories of the days spent with Keel, and was hurt—but sympathetic—when the doctor left him to take up a post with the World Health Organization. Such was their friendship that Steed still received cards from his old friend, and from time to time Keel's name would appear in the *Guardian*, linked to any number of goods deeds. Steed liked to think that Keel had learned something from him.

Finding a partner to replace Keel had taken a while, but the search had paid off handsomely. Investigating a group of men who were using the threat of black magic and voodoo to dig vital top-secret formulae from a group of boffins, Steed had been introduced to Mrs. Catherine Gale, an anthropologist working at the British Museum. Steed's initial reaction to her had definitely been more than slightly sexual, and she had quickly scented his interest and steered him well clear. While she was not a prude, she'd informed him, she most certainly didn't reciprocate his interest—a challenge that Steed couldn't resist. Having steered Mrs. Gale toward a restaurant—Italian, her favorite—he learned over dinner that she was trained in the martial arts and had an extensive knowledge of science, photography, criminology, and other fields. A germ of an idea had formed in Steed's head: if he could interest her in picking up where Keel had left off, it would be a case of let the baddies beware, and gung ho Mr. Steed. (He had always been overly enthusiastic in regard to a pretty face.) She signed on, and the partnership had lasted for two years of topsy-turvy, wham-bam escapades.

Finally, though, Cathy (as she preferred to be called) had elected to return to the quieter life. After a short American holiday—Steed had been astounded to receive a Christmas card from Cathy postmarked Fort Knox, of all places!—she had returned to her first love: Africa.

Studying the mating habits of anthropoids, recalled Steed with a smile as he steered the Bentley's nose onto Charing Cross Road. Remembering the entry in the *Guardian,* Steed smiled to himself—pity there wasn't really a gorilla on the loose in Surrey; Cathy would have been just the person to hunt it down. Probably would have gotten it into one of her peculiar oriental holds and forced it to cry out for mercy!

Replacing Cathy had been even a tougher task than replacing David Keel. Eventually, though, Steed's social contacts had paid dividends—a veritable jackpot, in fact, in the shapely form of Mrs. Emma Peel.

Hitting second gear and spinning the steering wheel to glide the Bentley through the dense London traffic, Steed thought back to their first meeting. A hint of a smile pursed his lips as he recalled the inauspicious start to their friendship. It had been at a party given by his industrial friend, Bertie Clivesdale, thrown to celebrate his good fortune at securing a winning bid for a Ministry of Defense contract. Steed's glass of Chivas Regal had been accidentally knocked from his hand by a passing waiter, and its entire contents cascaded over the back of Emma's innovative crepe-and-leather evening suit.

Aghast, Steed began, "My dear . . . ?"

"Mrs. Peel," she replied, smiling as she turned to face him. Steed had seen many beautiful women in his time, but the graceful poise and the arresting smile now turned upon him wiped away those memories. And in her gaze there was no hint of accusation for having ruined her attire. "Emma to my friends. Are *we* going to be friends?"

"But—your outfit . . . look, I'm terribly sorry, but the waiter—"

"Oh, that!" said Emma, her eyes twinkling as she looked down at her clothes. "It is really no problem. I always carry a second outfit, in case of such an emergency."

"Well, that's awfully kind of you." Pressing his luck, he added: "Look, this place appears to be getting crowded—and, between the two of us, Bertie's wife isn't renowned for her buffet prowess. Allow me to offer you dinner—to make amends. I know this little place just around the corner."

"There really is no need to make amends," she said, "Mister . . . ?"

"Steed. John Steed," he replied, his hopes falling.

"*John*. Give me five minutes, and I'll meet you at the door."

Two hours later, they were friends.

Like Mrs. Gale before her, Mrs. Peel's expertise in things usually considered—by the male domain, at least—to be the province of men, never ceased to amaze Steed. Her accomplishments were second to none. Equally proficient in the art of combat as Steed's previous partner, Mrs. Peel brought with her an air of irreverence, a vast supply of knowledge on seemingly endless subjects, and grace and charm in abundance. She lived for dangerous assignments, displaying initiative and skill whenever out in the field. She worked hand in glove with Steed, complementing his sometimes brash style. Together they had dealt with a seeming conveyor-belt line of weird and wacky—but thoroughly dangerous—villains. His one regret had been that she had never expressed anything stronger than affection for him. Good Lord, although Emma had frequently asked him to do so, he had never even called her by her Christian name, preferring instead to address her always as Mrs. Peel. And then along came her missing husband—and Steed said goodbye to *Emma*.

He returned to the present with a jolt. Spinning the Bentley's steering wheel, he managed to avoid the reckless rider who had crept up behind him on a Vespa motor scooter, attempting to pass the Bentley's sleek lines on the *inside* lane, by inches. When would these tearaways learn? Checking his wing mirror, he eased his foot down on the accelerator and glided with comfort past a red double-decker bus. Rolling his tongue across his teeth, he resisted the urge to check and see if Mother was aboard it.

Mother was the superior who had assigned him to work with Tara King, his current partner. For the first and only time, Steed had been assigned a partner, due to changes within the Department. Charles had retired and a new chief had been introduced. Mind you, Steed had *asked* for a replacement, secure in the knowledge that Mother knew his preferences. At first he had been somewhat resentful of the girl his superior had sent along, but he'd soon found Mother's choice to be perfect. True, she was a shade younger than he would have selected himself, but she quickly proved that she was a rugged fighter, possessed tenacity, was intelligent, and had a quirky free spirit. And—the icing on the cake—she found Steed physically attractive and was more than happy to share off-duty hours with him.

Mother had proven his soundness of judgment.

No one knew what his real name was—rumor had it that he had been a field operative during the War and had been wounded in France, but no one had ever discovered more. He fussed over his charges like a mother tending her flock, and so the operatives had taken to calling him this behind his back. One day he had overheard them using it—and liked it, adopting it as his nom de guerre. It was typical of Mother to enjoy the perversity of the joke.

The Department had run most efficiently in Mother's hands. Which raised the question in Steed's mind again—why this sudden summons out of the blue from *Charles*? And why Dawson Street, a place that hadn't been used for years?

In the world of espionage, danger is ever present, its deadly barbs aimed at those with knowledge and ability. Like Charles before him, Mother had changed the location of the organization's bases and contact points fairly frequently to avoid giving the opposition an easy shot at them. Charles had always favored the disguise of shops to hide the base of his operations. Dawson Street was a case in point, a dingy old bookstore in the heart of Soho, sandwiched between a music shop that attacked the hearing and a porno shop that attracted the eye.

Parking the Bentley, Steed noted that the bookshop appeared to be closed. Instinctively the thought that this might be a trap sprang to mind, and he approached the premises with caution. Charles's voice had been authentic, no doubt about it—but perhaps he had been speaking under duress?

Sidling to peer in the window, Steed cast a glance at the rows of books on display. Third book in, second row down . . . a sigh of relief eased through the corners of his mouth. Darwin's *Origin of Species*. Then Charles's call was really on the level. Had it been *Das Kapital*, Steed would have taken the back door—and watched out for flying bullets.

The bell over the door pinged as he stepped into the musty-smelling shop. Tall shelving surrounded him, stacked high with antiquarian hardcovers. Near the door was a pile of well-thumbed recent paperbacks, marked for sale at sixpence a copy. He peered at the top one. Another James Bond thriller; Double-O whatever had saved the world again. How they misled the reading public about the real world of spies. He passed on toward the counter, swinging his tightly furled umbrella aloft to land squarely on his right shoulder.

Charles sat there, reading the *Times Literary Supplement*. Once again, the correct signal that all was well. Glancing up, his one-time superior nodded and then carefully folded his paper and set it down on the counter, trying not to disturb the layer of dust.

"Charles, it's good to see you again," Steed said politely.

"Changed your opinion somewhat?" asked Charles gruffly, recalling the times he and Steed had embarked on head-to-head confrontations. Charles had been viewed by those who served under him as a pudgy father figure—until angered, when his celebrated temper would pour scorn on any operative not pulling his weight. It was inevitable that Steed—always his own man—and Charles would occasionally clash. They had done so, often, but Charles's respect for his junior had never dimmed. "I don't like this business, Steed. Not one little bit."

Clearing a chair of books, Steed sat in silence, waiting for Charles to tell him the worst.

"Trouble!" the short man barked. Turning, he dragged a dusty atlas down from the shelf behind him and from its pages extracted a red file. Opening its cover, he took out a photograph and passed it to Steed.

Steed glanced at it. The youngish face was familiar. "David Keller," he said. "One of the bright young things. He has a good off-spin when he bowls at cricket."

"Had," Charles modified. Steed raised an eyebrow and waited. Charles passed Steed a second photograph from the file. "He was killed last night."

This picture showed Keller's body. It was half in and half out of a wrecked telephone box. Steed's eyebrows rose further as he examined the signs of damage. The glass-and-metal box looked as if something had torn a hole in it. Keller's body left little to the imagination.

"A car?" Steed wondered aloud.

"Blow to the neck," Charles said, looking down at the autopsy report he had removed from the file. "One blow, instantly shattered the spine. Undoubtedly some form of metal weapon, which accounts for the twisted mess of the box. The killer must have smashed the glass first, then pulled Keller onto his knees before delivering the lethal blow."

"Odd," mused Steed, staring again at the photograph.

"It's worse than odd, Steed," snapped the other. "That's why you're being briefed by *me*. Why I was called away from my quiet home and my bees."

"And Mother?"

Ignoring Steed's question, Charles handed him the rest of the file. "Keller had been working on a case, Steed. Something about a double agent in the Department." He sighed and shook his head. "Keller was assigned to root him out. His daily reports are all there, but they didn't add up to much—until last night."

Steed nodded and turned another page. "Obviously, Keller found the mole, and the mole found Keller before he could talk."

"Something like that. Anyway, Keller called me very early this morning to say he'd made contact. Woke me up and puzzled me. I'm retired, have nothing to do with the case, so why would Keller call me—with an Alpha Priority code?" Reaching under the counter, Charles produced a portable tape recorder. "Luckily, old habits die hard. I started taping automatically. I soon found the answer—I discovered why he called me and not Mother."

Flicking a switch, he set the small spools in motion. Steed leaned forward to listen to the tape. He heard the sound of a scream, the shattering of broken glass, and then the blow. After a few seconds of silence, a voice: "I'm sorry, but your caller has been disconnected."

Steed slumped back in his chair. He could hardly believe his ears. He stared at Charles in shock. Charles simply nodded, confirming what they both already knew.

The voice had been undeniably Mother's.

3 Mother's Left Home—Steed's Gone Over

Reaching over, Steed switched off the tape recorder. Then, thoughtfully, he rewound the tape and played it a second time.

"There's no mistake," Charles said roughly. "It's Mother all right."

"It doesn't make sense," Steed replied. "*Mother?* I can't believe it."

"Believe it. The Minister does—that's why you're here."

Steed had an ugly idea of what would be coming next. "You mean . . . ?"

To avoid looking Steed in the eyes, Charles bent down to remove the rewound spool. "Confirm the information," he ordered, somewhat gruffly. "We have to assume that Mother has left home—and if it's true, then your orders are to terminate him."

Steed reached out and plucked the tape from Charles's hand. He looked at it accusingly, then slipped it into his jacket pocket. "That's not my style," he objected mildly.

"I know that, Steed," Charles agreed. "But . . . well, if Mother has been turned, then we need someone we can trust implicitly to eradicate the problem. You're the only one with utterly impeccable qualifications for the task. It has to be you, Steed, and you alone."

That wasn't a pleasant thought. "And Tara?" Steed prompted.

"She was handpicked by Mother," Charles said coldly. "Oh, I know that was some time ago, but if we can't trust Mother—"

"Then who can we trust?" Steed sighed, then smiled and tipped his hat. Rising, he crossed to the door. "I'll be in touch when I have news."

"Steed."

Pausing with his hand on the door handle, Steed looked back. Charles seemed very uncomfortable.

"Steed, do you remember the name of that man you interrogated back in 'sixty-four—the doppelganger?"

"Borowski."

"Quite right. I'm sorry."

"Perfectly understandable." Steed grinned, knowing what had prompted the question. "That reminds me, Charles. Do you still visit your Aunt May every summer? The one with the bull terrier named Corky?"

A smile of satisfaction crossed his superior's face. "Yes, I do. She's as fit as ever. I'm sorry about this,

Steed. I truly am. If there were any other way to handle this . . ."

"I know." Steed left.

Charles began sorting together the scattered photographs. He heard the Bentley start up before Steed drove off. A photograph of Mother slipped from the file and fluttered to the floor. Picking it up, Charles stared at it for a second, then slipped it back into the file. "I've done all I can for you," he muttered. "I only pray I've done the right thing." Sighing, he shuffled off into the back room, preparing to move on to his next hiding place.

Tara King yawned and stretched leisurely. It was one of those gloriously golden days when she had no assignment, and the weekend stretched ahead with promise—punting on the Thames, perhaps? A picnic in the New Forest? A run down to Brighton? Or simply theater and then dinner? Well, she could make up her mind any time at all. Reaching from under the bed covers, she groped for the white-and-gold antique-style telephone. Then she dialed Steed's home number.

There was no reply, which surprised her. Struggling to the surface of the covers, she looked at her clock. Just after twelve—he'd normally be drinking his third cup of tea by now. Unless he'd been called in for something—in which case, why hadn't she been? Odd, especially given Steed's ingrained habits.

Perhaps something was wrong? An opposition move against him? Perhaps he was in trouble? Or was she melodramatically interpreting an unanswered phone? He could have just stepped out for some other reason.

Better to be on the safe side. Slipping from beneath the sheets, she padded off for a shower. She'd just pop over to Stable Mews. If Steed had merely stepped out, then he could take her to lunch when he returned. If there was trouble . . .

With this in mind, she selected a culotte outfit that gave her plenty of freedom of movement. To complement its light green color, she wore a ruffled blouse of lemon silk. After a moment's thought, she slipped on her reinforced shoes with the metal-tipped toes. It made a good kick even more effective. She glanced at herself in the mirror. Her auburn hair looked fine, so she began brushing it out.

The telephone rang; smiling, she picked it up. Steed had decided to give her a call after all. "Hello."

She recognized the voice immediately. It wasn't Steed; it was Mother. "Miss King, the Hendon Way. Immediately." The line went dead.

Tara looked at the phone, puzzled. Hardly a normal summons, or Mother's usual manner. He had sounded very disturbed, angry, as though there was something weighty on his mind. But the Department had nothing on at the moment. Something *was* wrong. Why had Mother called her? Why not Steed?

Snatching up her handbag, she ran up the staircase and out of her two-level flat, then got into her sports car. With a screech of burning tires, she sped off toward the rendezvous point. Her brain racing faster than the car engine, she pictured all kinds of trouble. Was Steed in danger? It wouldn't be the first time—or the last. Was Steed missing? That wasn't altogether uncommon; he frequently dropped out of sight without leaving word of his whereabouts. Why *had* Mother sounded so worried?

She was unable to shake an intuitive feeling that there was bad news waiting for her. Since she had been working with Steed, she had encountered many things that were difficult to explain away rationally. Her senses had become finely tuned. She could smell trouble in an instant. Or was her intuition simply working overtime?

She drew up at the Hendon Way, to discover the parking lot virtually deserted. It was too early in the day for the regulars to have arrived yet. The place was very quiet, save for a group of youngsters sitting huddled in a corner of the lounge, arguing fiercely over the merits of their favorite television show. Crossing to the bar, she admired the cozy ambience of the pub—wooden paneling, plush seating, and fine prints on the wall. As she approached, the barman looked up from polishing glasses. He nodded toward one of the side doors, and Tara flashed him a grateful smile.

Passing through the door, she found herself in a small corridor. A door at the far end was marked PRIVATE. She pushed at it, and it opened onto what at first looked like another bar. A second examination showed that instead of beer pumps, the bar was lined with customized telephones. Instead of a barmaid, Rhonda stood at the ready. As ever, her face was completely impassive, revealing nothing behind her azure-blue eyes. She was Mother's bodyguard—a six-foot, four-inch blond Amazon. At the room's only table sat Mother.

Ageless in a way—he might be anywhere from forty to sixty—Mother was inclined to fat. Part of the reason for this was that he was confined to a motorized wheelchair, which he spun around to face Tara. His dark mustache twitched impatiently as he beckoned her over to the bar. There was no sign of Steed.

"Took your time getting here," Mother growled. "This is urgent, Miss King."

"Sorry, Mother," Tara apologized, although she had made the trip as fast as she could—and had broken several speeding restrictions to do so. At least she hadn't been ticketed; Mother hated his agents to get speeding tickets.

The man in the wheelchair held out his hand toward Rhonda. Reaching beneath the bar, she pulled out a file and passed it over. Mother tossed this onto the table and opened it. "Know him?" he asked, pointing at the photograph.

Leaning over his shoulder to examine it more closely, Tara nodded. "Yes. He was in my year at training school. Harrison—Damian Harrison, isn't it?"

"*Wasn't* it," Mother stressed. "He was killed last night."

Tara was sorry to hear this. Harrison had been a likable and efficient agent.

"He was looking into the reports that there's a double agent in the Department. Hardly a word in almost a month, then he called in last night. He rang from a railway station just outside London. Said he'd made contact, and then he was killed."

"Do we know by whom?" Tara asked, more as a matter of habit than because she expected an answer. To her surprise, Mother scowled.

"We do!" he snapped, holding out his hand again. This time Rhonda placed a tape recorder into it. "His killer left us in little doubt."

"Odd," Tara commented.

"More than odd," snapped Mother. Why was he so angry? "Listen."

He started the tape. They heard the swish of something striking Harrison, and then the clear, precise voice that said: "I'm sorry, but your caller has been cut off."

The voice belonged to John Steed.

Tara collapsed into a chair that Rhonda had thoughtfully swung into place behind her. In shock, she played back the tape again to be absolutely certain. Mother sat patiently through it, waiting until she switched off the machine. Her face ashen, Tara slammed down her finger on the stop button.

"*Steed*," she whispered. The name choked in her throat.

"Steed!" nodded Mother grimly.

"But it can't be. He—"

"Would never do such a thing," Mother interjected with a sigh. "It's hard to believe, but it's him. I've played it several times myself. The voice on the tape *is* Steed—there is absolutely no doubt."

"I refuse to believe it," said Tara, frowning. "It can't be! There has to be some mistake."

Mother waved his stick at the recorder. "There's no mistake. You heard the tape yourself. How could it be anyone *but* Steed?"

"But it can't be," Tara insisted. "A mimic, perhaps?"

Sighing, Mother sat back in his wheelchair. "My first thought. I had it checked against Steed's voice-print. The patterns match perfectly—too perfectly. Terrible as it is, Miss King, we must accept it: Harrison was killed by Steed."

"But . . . *Steed*," Tara insisted. "A double agent? I can't believe it. I refuse to accept the evidence, no matter what—"

"Then try!" growled Mother. "The Minister does. He's very perturbed by this. If Steed's gone over, then the whole Department is in jeopardy."

Tara was finding it difficult to contain the whirl of emotions within her. A voice in her head told her flatly that Steed could never be a traitor. Yet there was no denying that the voice on the tape was Steed's. Who knew the sound of it better than she? "So," she finally managed to get out, "what's our next move?"

"If Steed has defected," Mother said, "then who knows who else in the Department can be trusted?"

"Including me?" asked Tara wryly.

"*I* handpicked you, Miss King. Granted, I could be taking a chance, but I'm confident that you will prove the soundness of my judgment." He gestured with his cane at the tape recorder. "Steed would have allowed that to be made only if he were ready to leave. In which case, it is imperative that he be stopped. You are familiar with his habits. You must find him and ensure that he does not go over."

Tara's blood went cold. "Mother . . ." she whispered.

Mother looked back at her, confirming her worst

fears. "Yes. You may have to kill him to stop him."

Turning her head away, Tara lowered her eyes. She couldn't bear to think of the possibility. In training school, the instructors had always told her that *anyone* might prove to be a double agent—but Steed? Not Steed. Yet there was the tape. Spinning around, she took the tape from the machine and slipped it into her handbag. Then she stood up, looked down at Mother, and marched out of the room without a word.

Mother sighed again, deeply, and snapped the file closed. His eyes caught Rhonda's impassive face. "What else could I do?" he asked, reacting to her unspoken words. "I've given Steed the best chance he'll get. I pray that he accords Tara the same." He stared at the door glumly. "If Steed has turned rogue, then Miss King could well wind up being his next victim . . ."

With barely a blink of her eyes, Rhonda wheeled the fat man out of the room.

4 Doctor W. H. O.

David Keel awoke with a start, uncertain for a second where he was. A low glow from the bulb in the desk lamp told him he had fallen asleep working at his desk. Yawning, he pushed back his shirt cuff and glanced at his watch. Past noon already!

Brushing back the hair from his eyes, he stood up. The heavy curtains were still closed from last night. How long had he been working? Until three or four in the morning? He couldn't remember. He pulled back the curtains, wincing as daylight streamed into the small study. The room looked a mess. Revised papers covered the desktop, and his jacket had slipped from the back of his chair to the floor. A half-empty coffee mug sat alone by the ashtray, which was brimful of cigarette butts. Still, with the trip to Katawa being brought forward a month, there was too much work to get out of the way to worry about being tidy as well.

He walked to the kitchen, put the coffeepot on, then drew himself a burning-hot bath. Fifteen minutes later, he felt much better. Toweling his hair dry, he sipped at a steaming mug of coffee and felt alive again. Did he need a shave? Peering into the mirror, he stared at his rugged face. His eyes were lined with lack of proper rest. If the handsome, strong features had belonged to a patient, Dr. Keel would have prescribed rest. As it was, he had no time for that. The emergency in Katawa was getting worse. He had to get back to those reports, clear them, and be ready to fly out by the end of the week.

It was ironic, really. A month ago he had never heard of the country. When he had been given this assignment by the World Health Organization, he'd been forced to look the place up in an atlas. It was one of the small African nations that had just become independent and changed its name. The old colonial ties with England were still strong, though, and English was the official language. That helped, because Keel had never been much of a linguist. W.H.O. had become involved when a famine had exacerbated an outbreak of plague in the northeast of the country. Katawa's progressive Prime Minister, a jovial, intelligent man named M'Begwe, had immediately asked for help. W.H.O. had assigned Keel and Dr. Bennett Cowles to go check out the progress of the disease and suggest measures to combat it.

Keel had been asked to finish off the current batch of reports, and Cowles had kindly offered him a room in his own home. This pleased Keel, and he'd gladly accepted. Since joining W.H.O., Keel had hardly had the time to find a permanent residence. Cowles, a renowned genetic scientist, had a place just off Harley Street, which was more than convenient. It had also allowed Keel the opportunity to get to know his colleague better, since the two men had never met. Unfortunately, with Cowles winding up his university work and Keel preparing his reports and making arrangements for the trip, they had hardly found the time to socialize.

Speak of the devil! As Keel mused, the door opened and Cowles entered. He gave a cheery wave and hung up his coat and hat.

"Coffee?" Keel called. "Freshly made."

"Ah, already you know my weaknesses." Cowles laughed. "Please. Milk and two sugars." He entered the kitchen. Accepting the cup, he took a mouthful. "Ah! As a physician, I am aware that sugar is bad for you. As a coffee drinker, however, I refuse my own medical advice." He laughed again. "How are the reports coming along?"

"Slowly," Keel growled. "But I'll beat them before the end of the week, even if I have to bury the last of them in the garden."

Cowles's eyes twinkled. He was everyone's image of the jolly little fat man; his cheeks were red with continual laughter, his ample paunch restrained somewhat by a belt. His hair was thinning, and he had a habit of running his hand through what remained, as if constantly checking that he wasn't yet bald. He was a ferociously capable research geneticist, however, with a string of complex papers and discoveries to his name. He would be a valuable aide in Katawa, checking on the genetic factors of this new disease, which seemed to be incredibly selective in choosing its victims. The natives of the neighboring countries seemed entirely unaffected.

"I, too," Cowles laughed, "am having my problems with getting down to my work. The university was more than happy to grant me a leave of absence, but my graduate students are not so understanding. Each of them, it seems, thinks that he will get his doctorate only if I am standing there brooding over him like a mother hen." He shook his head in mock sorrow. "Ah, the youth of today. Still, it is nice to feel wanted, is it not, David?"

Keel helped himself to a second cup. "Believe me, we certainly are wanted." He gestured to the newspaper he had started to glance at. "The plague is spreading at an alarming rate."

"Yes, it seems that—"

He broke off as the doorbell rang. Frowning, he put down his cup. "Now, if that's another of my students, I shall be very perturbed!" He winked as he said it, and then headed for the front door.

As he turned the lock, someone shoved it open, slamming Cowles forcibly backward into the wall. His breath huffed out as he slammed against the plaster. Three men pushed their way into the hallway. Each of them wore a stockinette mask and was armed with a revolver. Keel stared at them in astonishment, and they seemed to be equally surprised to see him.

"A little early for Halloween," murmured Keel.

"Cripes," the first man muttered. "I thought this geezer lived alone. Now what, Marty?"

The heavily built Marty was obviously the leader

of the trio. His pale-blue, watery eyes flickered to Cowles and then to Keel. His revolver came up. "Nothin'," he said firmly. "As long as we don't have a hero here."

The other two men had their guns trained on Cowles. The doctor had lost all of his geniality now, and his face had gone gray. "What—what—" he tried to say, but a gun waved under his nose shut him up.

"Quiet, Pops," the thug said. "Then there won't be no trouble. You're takin' a little trip, is all. If you're real good, you'll even stay alive."

"Can it, Alfie," Marty muttered, eyeing Keel. "Take him out to the car."

Alfie and his companion prodded Cowles with their guns, and the doctor stumbled along with them and out the door. Marty's eyes never left Keel. When the two of them were alone, the thug moved forward. "On the floor," he ordered. Keel remained standing. "Down!" barked Marty, gesturing with his gun.

This was the opening that Keel had been hoping for. As the barrel of the gun moved sideways, he flung the coffee mug directly into the masked man's face. Marty moved to block the hurtling object, and Keel dived into action. Old habits die hard. His years working with Steed had not been wasted. Marty batted the cup to the floor, where it shattered, but Keel's jump took him down.

Both men hit the linoleum hard. Snapping out his arm, Keel grabbed Marty's gun hand and slammed it against the floor. The masked man grunted with pain, and Keel repeated the blow, feeling Marty's fingers loosen their grip slightly.

The thug attempted to punch Keel with his free hand, but Keel blocked the blow, then grabbed Marty's neck and squeezed.

The gun suddenly skidded free, across the slippery floor. Keel tightened his grip, but Marty shifted tactics, bringing up his knee to connect solidly with Keel's midriff. The doctor grunted in pain, and Marty wriggled loose of the strangling grip. Keel grabbed again, and the two men struggled. Something ripped, and Keel's fingers came free.

Marty struggled into a sitting position and punched outward. The blow caught Keel in the stomach and he groaned. He lashed out with his right, smacking a good blow into Marty's teeth. Pain shot up Keel's arm—a badly placed punch! Marty yelped and came at Keel again.

Pressing home his advantage, Keel brought up his leg and slammed it down on Marty's hand as the masked man tried to rise. The thug howled and then struck out. Ready now to finish the fight, Keel prepared a punch to Marty's unprotected jaw. Before he could deliver it, he felt a tremendous pain in his neck, and then blackness overtook him.

Alfie pushed Keel's unconscious body off his boss and grinned down at the butt of his gun. "Never fails, Marty," he observed, helping his friend up. "There's always a smartass."

Marty, aware of his failure to deal with Keel alone, was not in a good mood. "Yeah," he grunted, and retrieved his fallen gun. His hand hurt where Keel's heel had bruised him. He brought the barrel of the revolver to bear on the unconscious doctor.

Alfie pushed it aside. "If you plug 'im, Marty, then 'ool tell the cops that we snatched the doc?"

Marty considered the point and then nodded. "I owe him one, though." Crossing to Keel's body, he delivered a vicious kick into the unconscious man's ribs. Keel groaned and clawed at the floor. "He'll remember me." The thug grinned. He moved to put his gun in his pocket, and then swore. "Damn! The clown ruined my jacket!" The jacket, torn in the fight, had a large strip ripped out of it down the left-hand side.

Alfie grinned. "Don't worry, Marty," he said, trying to hide his amusement. "The money we're gettin' for this snatch'll buy you a 'undred more."

With a final scowl at Keel's unconscious form, Marty followed Alfie out and slammed the door.

Keel struggled awake again, this time with a searing pain in his neck and another in his ribs. Gathering his wits, he tentatively fingered the swelling lump on his neck, wincing as he touched it. A professional blow from behind. That was what had ended the fight.

With a start, his memory of the events returned. Cowles had been kidnapped! He rubbed his eyes, groaning with pain. Rolling gently over onto his back, he felt at the burning in his chest. He felt as though he'd been kicked in the ribs by a mule. Opening his shirt, he saw a large purpling area of skin. He *had* been kicked in the ribs; the mule had undoubtedly been called Marty. Gingerly, he tried to rise, but his head started swimming. Slowly, slowly. Overdo it and you'll pass out again. Easing himself over onto his hands and knees, he stayed there for a moment until the flashing yellow pain faded from his eyes.

Under the table he saw a piece of torn fabric and something white. He recalled a sound of ripping during the fight and pictured his hands tearing at Marty's coat. Carefully he urged his body forward and reached out to pick up whatever had fallen there. Then, feeling more confident, he used a nearby chair to haul himself onto his feet.

Fighting rising nausea and a giddy sensation in his head, he staggered into the hallway. His vision was still blurred, but he could make out the telephone on the stand there. It took him two attempts to pick up the receiver, though, and he could feel himself fading in and out of reality as he dialed 999. A cheery voice answered almost immediately, and he managed to get out his name and address, and then fell back against the wall. He managed to replace the phone in its cradle, and then sat there, breathing gently until his eyes could focus again.

He was gripping something in his left hand. For a moment he couldn't think what it could be, and then he remembered the whatever-it-was he had picked up from the kitchen floor. He opened his hand and stared at the object.

It was a card of some kind, made from plastic. It was about four inches long and three wide. Down the left edge was a metallic strip. Across the top were two words:

KNIGHT INDUSTRIES

Now what could this be? With a shrug that hurt his ribs, he put the card carefully into his pocket. Then he settled back to wait for the police to arrive.

5 "Bad Habits Die Hard, Major Steed"

There were, Steed knew, two ways of locating Mother. The first and most obvious was to simply call the contact number he had, and thus learn Mother's latest hideout. He ruled this out because it would alert Mother that he was on his way. If Mother had gone over, this would put him on his guard. It was also possible that Mother had already pulled up his roots and begun the process of fleeing.

Which left the second method of finding out where Mother was: ask the opposition.

The Soviet Embassy maintained a house in one of the quieter suburbs of London. Its ostensible purpose was to allow the bureaucrats a chance to escape from their work for a weekend. In fact, as Steed well knew, it was the headquarters of the KGB's English division. Steed parked the Bentley in the narrow lane behind the wall surrounding the house and took a small parcel from the backseat. Vaulting onto the vehicle's hood, he hooked his umbrella over a conveniently low tree limb overhanging the wall. A hop, and he was over and down into the bushes beyond.

As expected, barely had his feet touched the ground when six large Siberian wolfhounds hurtled around the corner of the house and headed straight for him. Steed quickly unwrapped his package, and the dogs all ground to a halt as he tossed six large, bloodred steaks onto the grass. Duty fought a short war with hunger, and the latter won. The dogs were kept permanently hungry to make them meaner, and this rare treat was too much for them. Warily watching him, they proceeded to gulp down the meat in large chunks. Steed smiled at them disarmingly, one eye on his wristwatch.

"Three, two, one . . ." He looked up expectantly. Right on "zero," the dogs began to yawn, then keeled over, fast asleep. "Like a charm," Steed murmured. The lab boys had done it again—tasteless, fast-acting tranquilizers. These little darlings would be out for a good thirty minutes, more than enough time for what he had in mind.

He moved from cover to cover, eventually reaching the terrace surrounding the large house. The building had once been the home of a wealthy squire who rode frequently to hounds. As a result, it was open to the grounds in a number of places. The terrace could be reached from the house through large French windows, Steed's chosen means of entry. Pausing outside the beautiful lead-glass doors, he examined them for signs of the inevitable alarm. He was somewhat professionally shocked to discover the wire led to an old-style box on the wall above the doors. Aware that the Russians eschewed much modern technology as decadent and bourgeois, he was nevertheless surprised that their budget wouldn't stretch to installing a better safety contraption than this. Why, they were almost inviting the denizens of Wormwood Scrubs into the place and offering them tea, crumpets, and their choice of loot! Steed was about to pry open the box and disconnect the alarm when a second thought crossed his mind. Peering closely at the red alarm box, his lips cracked into a smile.

"Ingenious," he murmured. "Disconnecting the wire actually triggers the alarm. They are getting better." Still, there was one point that the mastermind behind the safety device had overlooked—if the intruder *didn't* disconnect the wire, then the alarm was dead, and thus opening the doors was perfectly safe.

Cracking open the lock, he eased back the doors and slipped into the study. As Steed had half expected, the genius behind the alarm system waited within.

Brodny was sitting cross-legged in the center of the plush carpet, reading. In his early fifties, Brodny was almost totally bald—the sole hair on his head being a luxuriant growth over his upper lip. It was his personal homage to his hero, Josef Stalin. Tweaking this mustache from time to time, Brodny was so intent on studying the page of ciphers that he failed to hear the intruder's footsteps behind him.

A half grin crossing his face, Steed swept across

the room and laid the ferrule of his umbrella on Brodny's shoulder. The Russian leaped into the air with a squeal. Attempting to spin around and face his attacker gracefully, he managed to tangle his legs and sprawled helplessly on the carpet. Glaring, he looked up at the smiling face of Steed.

"Major Steed! You shouldn't do that!" he exclaimed. "I have a cardiac condition!"

"Dear me," Steed sympathized. "Really? Then I promise to send flowers to the funeral. Forgive me, old friend, but I was forced to bypass your burglar alarm."

Levering himself back to his feet, Brodny straightened out his suit and then his black tie. His hand smoothed nonexistent hair. His fears of imminent death were laid to rest; Steed had never been known to be violent without due provocation. At least, not yet. "Burglar alarm," he repeated. "But . . . how did you get past it?"

"A breeze," Steed smiled. "I simply didn't touch it."

Brodny thought this through and scowled. "But that is not playing the game," he complained. "You are *supposed* to disconnect it. Then, when you open the door, we catch you."

"And if I don't want to be caught?" Steed replied, his eyes twinkling at Brodny's frustration. "If I only want to talk?"

"If it's about the Southampton affair," the Russian began hastily, "that was not my—"

"It's not about the Southampton affair." Steed had no idea what Brodny was referring to, but filed the information away for future use. "It's about Mother."

"Yours or mine?" Brodny asked.

"Mine."

"Good." Brodny had sold out his own mother to the Party. She had been decadent and reactionary, and had beaten him frequently when he was a boy. He wondered, idly, if she was still in the Gulag. Crossing to his large oak desk, Brodny indicated a decanter and glasses. "Vodka?"

"How kind. Just a small one, please."

"So." Brodny poured the clear liquid into two glasses, his back to Steed. "What is it that you wish to know about your Mother? What could we possibly tell you that you do not already know?" As he spoke, he slipped a small bottle from an inside pocket and shook several drops into Steed's glass. There was a short-lived milkiness, then the vodka turned clear once more. Picking up the glasses, he smiled to himself. Turning, he offered Steed the doctored drink.

Smiling genially, Steed raised the glass. "Cheers." Then, placing the glass to his lips, he shook his head sadly and lowered his hand. "Brodny, old friend, it's really not polite to poison your visitors. I'm sure the maids must object to having to sweep out all of the corpses."

"Poison?" Brodny squeaked guiltily. "Comrade Steed, are you suggesting that I, Vladimir Yurislav Brodny, would—"

"That you did," Steed amended. "Perhaps you'd care to exchange glasses." He proffered the one he held.

Sweating, Brodny shook his head. "Well, perhaps in a moment of weakness I might have . . ." His strained voice trailed off under the unwavering smile Steed had turned upon him. He hastily put his own glass back on the tray. "I assure you, it was a reflex action only. Bad habits die hard, Major Steed. No offense intended."

"And none taken," Steed assured him, slapping the Russian heartily on the back. "Now, to show that there's no ill feeling on either part, why not let me have the information that I require?"

Brodny's mustache twitched. "Then you really are serious about the location of your superior?"

"I am."

"But surely you know where he is. Why come to me?"

"Call it a test," Steed suggested.

Shrugging, Brodny crossed to the wall safe, his mind racing. He would never understand the workings of the British mind, no matter how long he was stationed here. Carefully shielding the dial from Steed's view, he started to work on the lock. Behind him, Steed quietly switched the vodka glasses around and tipped a little powder into the one containing his drink. As he suspected, there was a slight yellowing as the antidote worked on the drink. It would leave the vodka with a bitter taste, but the drink was harmless now.

At the safe, Brodny was having trouble with the combination. The tumblers tweaked and turned, but the safe remained obstinately closed despite his efforts. He'd never been very good with numbers. Finally he gave up and looked at the cuff of his shirtsleeve, where he'd jotted the combination down. His memory refreshed, he opened the safe in seconds, making a great display of his dexterity in the process. Extracting a thin red file, he turned back to Steed.

"To show that we Russians can cooperate," he murmured diplomatically. Opening the folder, he placed it on his desk. "Naturally, I am not allowed to show you this document, but if you were to perhaps take a look while my back is turned . . . ?"

"Quite," Steed agreed. Brodny was definitely one of the eccentrics in this spy game. Steed wondered if he would ever understand the Russian mind. He examined the top piece of paper in the file. It was written, naturally, in Russian, but as he was fluent in the language, Steed had no problem translating it. After a moment, he glanced up and tipped his bowler to Brodny. "Thank you. Now I really must be going."

"A pleasure to see you, Major Steed." Brodny was all smiles as he escorted Steed back to the French windows. "I'd invite you to drop in any time, but you know how it is."

"Naturally," Steed agreed. "Your superiors might wonder why a known spy was calling on their, ah, cultural attaché." Nodding, he slipped out of the house.

Then, realization dawning, Brodny called out to him: "Major Steed—the dogs?"

As Steed vanished across the lawn, his voice floated back: "Sleeping like newborn puppies."

Grunting to himself, Brodny fastened the windows again. He had to admit that he liked Steed—oh, the man was a dirty capitalist pig, but he was a *charming* dirty capitalist pig. Every Christmas, Steed always sent him a magnum of champagne, and Brodny appreciated the thought. In return, he never missed sending Steed a small bomb in the mail. A gesture of respect between two adversaries. Yes, Steed was a good sort—but very, very unnerving.

What was this business about? He couldn't make any sense of it. Why should Steed come looking for such odd information? Distracted, the Russian picked up a glass of vodka and raised it at the huge, frowning portrait of Lenin. Then he downed it in a single gulp and sent the glass crashing into the empty fireplace.

Seeing the second glass sitting on the tray, he remembered the poison. Had he drunk from the right glass? Or, perhaps, had Steed switched the glasses while he had been opening the safe? Had he drunk vodka—or poison?

Panicking, he started to breathe deeply. Grabbing his wrist, he tried to time his pulse. At first he felt nothing and was afraid he was already dead. Then he managed to find the beat and closed his eyes, timing the throbs. It felt normal, so far. It felt—

There was a hand on his shoulder, and he shrieked. Spinning about, he adopted a karate stance, and wrenched his back. Groaning, he straightened up again and found himself staring into the wide-eyed, pretty face of Tara King.

"Did I pick a bad moment?" she asked politely. "You don't look too well."

"I may have broken my back," he mumbled, rubbing hard at it. His mind raced. What was going on? First Steed, and now his partner . . .

"Here," Tara said. "Allow me." Slipping behind him, she grabbed the collar of his jacket and heaved. Brodny squealed, but then felt a wonderful elation as she began to massage his back. In seconds, he felt fine, and barely more than half his current age.

"Mmmmmmm," he said, enjoying the feeling. Then, sadly, it stopped. Shaking his head, he blinked at her. "Is there a reason you are here?"

"Yes." Tara nodded, and walked around the desk. "I need a little information from you."

"You too?" Brodny was feeling more perplexed by the moment. "What am I, the information desk at Harrods? Or have I overlooked the fact that this week is open house for foreign agents? I protest. I do not work for British Intelligence. I work for the KGB!" Standing erect, he tugged his jacket back up, attempting to retain his dignity.

"Really?" Tara looked innocently amazed. "I thought that you were the cultural attaché here."

Caught, Brodny squirmed. "That too," he agreed. "But we have few secrets from one another."

"Then let's make it one less," she suggested brightly. "Why don't you tell me where I can find Steed?"

"Steed?" Brodny was now helplessly aflounder. "Do you think I could be taken in so easily? We Russians know a trick when we see one." Pointing at Tara, he laughed. "Ah, I see it now—you two are trying to make me lose my razor-sharp mind, and thus irreparably hamper Soviet espionage! Steed said it was a test."

"Steed! You mean he was here?"

"Of course. You know he was. Barely minutes ago. And also looking for information."

"On how to defect?"

Brodny laughed. "Ah, the English sense of humor! Steed—*defect?* Ha! Sooner would the glorious Party adopt the Pope as our leader." He gestured toward the still-open file on his desk. "He wanted to know where to find Mother."

It was Tara's turn to look puzzled. "He came here for that?"

"And to share a drink with an old comrade."

Resisting the thought that Steed had really gone over to the opposition—and was aiming to target Mother first—Tara glanced down at the file, and stiffened. "Is this report a joke?" she asked.

"Joke?" Brodny bridled at the suggestion. "We Russians *never* joke about espionage, Miss King. The information is barely hours old. Why should it be a joke?"

"Because it states here that Mother is aboard a submarine at Henley-on-Thames."

Nodding, Brodny crossed to join her. "Is that not correct?"

"No." Aware that Mother was in Hendon Way, Tara asked herself why, then, would the Russians have prepared a report stating that he was in Henley? And aboard a submarine, of all places? This case was getting stranger all the time. But it was clear that Steed thought Mother was in Henley. He might even be on his way there right now.

Brodny peered down at his report in annoyance. "This is all some elaborate trick you're playing, isn't it?" he said accusingly. "Admit it, Miss King, you and Steed are trying to outfox the master. It won't work."

"Not us." Tara smiled, crossing to the French

windows. "But perhaps someone is playing elaborate tricks on us all?" She gave him a mocking salute and then was gone. A second later, her head reappeared. "By the way, you've got the laziest guard dogs I've ever seen. If you'll take a tip from me, get some new ones." She vanished again, more permanently this time.

Puzzled, Brodny grabbed up the report and tore it into shreds. "Heads will roll for this!" he exclaimed. Then he threw the pieces onto the floor and jumped on them. Finally, he glanced back at his desk and saw the lone vodka glass.

The poison! He'd completely forgotten about it! Still, he was alive, which meant that he hadn't drunk the wrong glass after all! He'd better dispose of the other, before—

The door opened and Comrade Yosenka marched in. A lean, brooding eagle of a man, Yosenka was the Deputy Director of Espionage, though his official cover was as a chauffeur. Brodny never knew if he should salute the man or not. Glaring at Brodny, Yosenka caught sight of the glass of vodka.

"Drinking, comrade?" he hissed. "The Party disapproves of drunkenness."

"Yes, Comrade Yosenka," Brodny stammered. "But, you see—"

"Drunkenness will not be tolerated!" Yosenka glared at the quivering Brodny. Then, before Brodny could react, he picked up the vodka and downed it in a gulp. He tossed the glass into the fireplace and then stared back at Brodny, perplexed. "What is wrong with you, comrade? You've gone as pale as a bankrupt capitalist!"

Gulping back a croak, Brodny could do nothing but tremble. How did these things happen to him? And how could he tell Yosenka that he had just been accidentally poisoned?

It was definitely not Brodny's day.

6 Gale Force

Sighing, Cathy Gale pushed the papers away from her, then yawned and stretched. She brushed her mop of honey-blond hair back from her eyes and glanced up at the clock. After two already! She'd been wading through the proposals and official documents for almost six hours! No wonder she felt exhausted, thirsty, irritable. And she was barely halfway down the documents she'd promised herself that she'd get done today. The fight between stomach and conscience was brief. Pushing her chair away from the solid oak desk, she padded off toward the kitchen.

Purchased six months earlier, Cathy's house was deep enough into the Surrey countryside so she could forget that London even existed, but close enough for trips into town when they were necessary. An old mansion house, it had been sold off by some impoverished family almost a century ago, and had passed through many hands since then. It was probably too big for one person living on her own, but Cathy had fallen in love with the place.

Aside from her voluminous study, the ground floor contained a spacious dining room, a fully equipped kitchen, and a pleasant sitting room. Upstairs were her own bedroom, two guest rooms—originally there had been four, but Cathy had converted two into her photographic workshop-laboratory—and a small, boxy room that she'd turned into a library. A compact and comprehensive collection of anthropology books filled the room. Filing cabinets were crammed with her notes and photographs.

Right now, though, Cathy's mind was on the pantry and feeding the gnawing in her stomach. She helped herself to cheese, fresh bread, and—after a momentary pause—a glass of white wine. Passing back into the kitchen, she made herself comfortable and sank her teeth into her sandwich.

She luxuriated in the break from the papers, knowing she'd be back at them very shortly. They were too important to ignore for more than ten minutes or so. Prime Minister M'Begwe of the emerging African nation of Katawa had quite literally made her an offer she couldn't refuse.

Lost in her thoughts, she took another bite of the sandwich, followed by a sip of the wine. Three years earlier, she had said her farewell to Steed and headed back to Africa to spend six months observing mountain gorillas in their habitat. Within days, she had been deeply moved both by their characters and their plight. As the human race expanded, the gorillas were dying out—slowly, but inevitably. She had compared notes with Dr. Leakey on the subject, and shared his worries about the anthropoids' future.

The six months were over all too soon, and her life moved on, but she had never forgotten that concern. The past few years had left her with very little time to devote to anthropology, but recently she had reaffirmed her commitment and begun the fight to save the huge anthropoids. Finally, barely two months ago, she had managed to achieve a degree of success.

Katawa had been an old British colony just inland of the Gold Coast. For almost a century, the Empire had held sway there. Then, within the last two years, Katawa had finally won its independence, and M'Begwe was elected its first Prime Minister.

Cathy had known M'Begwe in their days as students in London, and recently his ambassador had contacted her with an offer to set up a gorilla sanctuary in his country. Naturally, she had jumped at the prospect, and they had talked it through. What she hadn't anticipated was the resistance to the idea, and the incredible struggle for funding. Despite M'Begwe's enlightened attitudes, many of his ministers believed that Katawa should spend its money on improving the lot of the inhabitants, not the wildlife. M'Begwe was convinced that a wildlife park would attract tourists, and he knew that a few hundred rich Americans passing through each year would work wonders for the economy. He had handed Cathy the problem of proving that the park reserve could work—and finding further backers.

She was almost ready now to present him with her findings. She had talked a number of millionaires—both British and American—into backing the initial phases of the scheme. She had the papers for the various grants worked out, and the blueprints for the building work had been produced. She even had estimates of the staff, supplies, and medicines that would have to be transported into the roadless mountain regions.

Her mind wandered for a moment. She was moving a mountain of paperwork, she realized, to save a mountain of gorillas. She *was* achieving her goal, however. Just a few more days and she'd be ready to fly out and present her case before the Katawan parliament.

Finishing off her lunch, she started back toward her study. The doorbell rang and she changed course, crossing the highly polished parquet hall to the massive oak doors. She was ready in case of any emergency—her time with Steed having taught her to maintain at all times a small-caliber pistol within reach of the front door. She eased back the wrought-iron bolts and swung open the door. A policeman stood out there, his bicycle propped up against one of the stone lions that flanked the entranceway. She smiled politely, but inquisitively.

The officer touched his gloved hand to his helmet and smiled back—friendly but businesslike. "Afternoon, ma'am. Mrs. Gale?"

"Yes. What's wrong? Do come in."

"Thank you, ma'am." He marched in and sat somewhat self-consciously on a chair. He shifted from side to side, as if uncertain how to explain his presence.

Cathy tried to put him at ease. "How may I help you? Is there a problem, Constable?" she asked, settling herself into a high-backed chair opposite him.

"No, ma'am, not as such." He took a breath and tried again. "Inspector Wallace asked me to call."

"Harry?" Cathy recalled the man well; he and his wife often attended Church Hall charity events, and she had had more than one conversation with him. A pleasant enough man, if a trifle lacking in imagination. A good, solid British policeman. "In connection with?"

"Er . . . it's just that . . ." His voice trailed off again, as if he was at a loss for inspiration. "The Inspector wondered . . . er . . ."

"Yes?" Cathy prompted.

"Apes, ma'am."

"Pardon?" Surprised by the word, Cathy raised an eyebrow. "Apes?"

"Yes, ma'am. You wouldn't happen to *own* one, would you?"

"Good heavens, no!" At a loss to understand this conversation, Cathy stared at the uncomfortable policeman. "Would you like to search the house to see if one is nesting in the roof timbers?"

"No, ma'am, that won't be necessary," the constable replied. His cheeks turned crimson as he looked at Cathy again. "Well, this might sound odd, Mrs. Gale, but the Inspector believes he's been tracking one, just half a mile down the road."

"In *Surrey*, Constable?" It finally clicked home in Cathy's memory. "Ah, the killer gorilla that the papers have been full of? The one that the police claim *doesn't* exist?"

"That's right, ma'am," the constable agreed, relieved she'd caught on at last. Oddly enough, he didn't seem at all perturbed about the inherent contradiction in the Inspector hunting for a gorilla that didn't exist. "Can't have the populace getting hot under the collar about apes roaming the countryside."

"Of course not," Cathy replied. "It's all right to have the odd dead body littering the countryside, but not panic in the streets." Leaning across to her desk, Cathy slid a cigarette out of the box lying there. She offered one to the policeman, who declined. Flicking open her lighter, she lit up and then inhaled deeply, blowing smoke into the air. "*Is* there a killer ape on the loose?"

Once again the officer fumbled for words. "Possibly, ma'am, but we don't want to admit it. Imagine what the press would do with a story like that. That's why the Inspector asked me to call. He remembered that you know something about gorillas."

Cathy's eyebrow lifted again. "Well, yes, just a little."

"The Inspector wondered if you'd care to join him, Mrs. Gale. To offer advice."

"About?"

"Capturing the runaway—if it exists," the policeman added, showing a trace of skepticism. "He has already called in a couple of marksmen."

Cathy was appalled. "He intends to *kill* it?"

"It's already killed two innocent bystanders, ma'am," the policeman said by way of confirmation.

"And will probably kill more—if provoked!" Cathy exclaimed. Crushing out her cigarette in the ashtray, Cathy asked the officer to wait for a moment. Leaving the poor fellow to gather his thoughts, she stormed up the stairs and into the library. From a case on the wall she took down her rifle and cocked its firing mechanism. Perfect working order, as she had known it would be. Grabbing a handful of darts and a shoulder bag, she ran back down the stairs, cramming the darts into the bag. The policeman eyed her curiously.

"What are those for, ma'am?" he asked.

"Protection and security." She smiled. "They're tranquilizer darts. Guaranteed to bring down a bull elephant." Seeing the man still staring, she explained: "*If* the ape exists, I don't want to see it killed—or wounded—by your so-called marksmen."

"They're the best in the force, ma'am—they could hit a rabbit at a hundred yards."

"But they're not stalking rabbits, are they, Constable? If there really is a gorilla, I assure you they will need help—expert help. Isn't that what Inspector Wallace wants me for?"

"Well, yes, ma'am. But the gun . . . er, I'm not sure the Inspector would like that, ma'am."

"Believe me, he will—when he sees what he is up against."

The policeman didn't have to think that one over for long. Glum-faced, he nodded and headed for his bike. Seeing the officer donning his bicycle clips, Cathy called to him:

"The motor will be quicker. Hop in." She crossed to the Land Rover parked in the driveway and threw the rifle and satchel inside it onto the passenger seat. The constable climbed in as best he could. Cathy sent the vehicle shooting forward with a roar down the driveway toward the exit gate. Pebbles flew up from beneath its tires. Navigating a sharp right turn, Cathy sped off down the quiet country lane.

Exactly ninety seconds later, they arrived at the search site.

Wallace's car and two black police transit vans were parked by the road. All three were empty. Stepping out of the Land Rover, Cathy retrieved her rifle and satchel. The policeman gestured across a small potato field toward a line of trees. "They're over there, ma'am," he told her. Slinging the rifle over one shoulder and the bag of darts over the other, Cathy followed him across the furrowed field.

She could see the tracks of several men underfoot. Police boots, she noted—inevitably in large sizes. Why did policemen always seem to have such big feet? Several of the growing potato plants had had their stems broken by the passage of the men. The farmer wouldn't like that, thought Cathy; then again, he probably preferred a few ruined potatoes to a giant ape on the loose.

Wallace and his men were just inside the woods, all armed with large sticks. Two of the constables wore flak jackets and carried rifles, casually held at the ready. Suppressing a smile, Cathy joined the Inspector.

"Mrs. Gale, thank you for coming," Wallace greeted her. "A rum lot, this one. The constable has filled you in?"

"About the gorilla? Do you believe in it, Harry?"

"Dunno. There's something in there," he told her, pointing toward the dense undergrowth a few yards ahead of them. "*What* it is, I can't say yet. But it's a killer, and we have to bring it in before there's more deaths."

"Take my word for it, Harry," she told him grimly, gesturing at the officers in flak jackets, "someone *will* be killed if you allow those men to go after it with their toy pistols."

"Toy pistols? Those men are armed with the best we've got. Those rifles would stop an elephant."

"I can tell you've never tried them on one," Cathy said dryly. "You need something more powerful than that. Something like this." Shrugging the rifle off her shoulder, Cathy proceeded to load one of the darts into its breech. "This one's been specially adapted to fire these tranquilizer darts. They will sedate the beast for hours, and we can get London Zoo to send us a cage out for it."

Wallace frowned. "I don't like the idea of trying to *catch* a murdering animal," he objected.

"Whatever happened to 'innocent until proven guilty'?" she asked him. "Or does that apply only to humans? Harry, if there is a gorilla, you have no proof that it's responsible for the deaths."

Wallace grunted and drew his raincoat closer about him. "Proof?" he echoed. "Well, if you want proof, take a look at this." He led the way to a small pathway through the bushes and brambles and pointed dramatically. "There's your proof."

Cathy bent down to get a better view. There was no doubt in her mind that it was a gorilla spoor. A trail of the prints—probably only hours old—led into the trees. Yet there was something odd about the prints. She frowned, trying to place them. Nothing came to her.

"We've followed them about a hundred yards so far," Wallace said, leaning over her shoulder. "Are they, in your expert opinion, gorilla tracks?"

"Yes," she replied absently. She touched the edge of one print and then stood up. Why did it seem wrong to her? "But there's something I don't understand. Where could a gorilla have come from? I presume you've checked to see if there's a circus in town? Checked with London Zoo for an escapee?"

"Of course," growled the policeman. "A dead end. Perhaps someone was keeping it as a pet. They're a rum lot around here, you know. I wouldn't put anything past them. If it escaped, the owner may be too scared to report it."

"Hardly likely, is it?" Cathy scoffed.

"Perhaps not," Wallace bristled, "but how else can you explain those tracks?"

"I can't," Cathy replied, raising the rifle to her breast. "But if there *is* a gorilla out there, I'll find it for you."

The Inspector blocked her way, an adamant expression on his face. "I really can't let you go looking for that thing alone. It's much too dangerous. Perhaps a couple of my men—"

"Inspector," Cathy replied, all familiarity now gone from her voice, "take my word for it. I'll be a damned sight safer *without* having to worry about your men. In Africa, I was close enough to smell them, and—" She broke off as she finally realized what her subconscious had figured out. "The scent!"

"What about it?" Wallace asked, sniffing the air.

Cathy bent again to examine the spoor. Scooping up a handful of dirt, she waved it unceremoniously under Wallace's nose. "What can you smell?"

"Compost," he grunted, turning away.

"But *not* gorilla," she finished, wiping off her hands on her jacket. "That's what's wrong—there's no gorilla scent."

Wallace shrugged. "Maybe he's a cleanliness freak and takes a bath every morning. What difference does it make?"

Cathy shook her head in disgust. Alarm bells were ringing in the back of her mind. Missing pet, indeed. How did the police ever solve a crime? She wished she were near a phone right now; she knew just the person to call for advice. But Steed believed—as she wished him to—that she was still in Africa.

Steed! She'd been trying to put that kindly rogue out of her thoughts for the past three years. Amazing how his name still sprang to mind!

Wallace misinterpreted her thoughtfulness as acquiescence. He gently took her arm. "Just go back to your car, Mrs. Gale," he suggested. "We can manage quite well without—"

She shook off his hand. "Inspector, please allow me to do as I suggest. It could well mean the difference between . . ."

Her words trailed away as she sensed a motion in the trees. She spun around and then froze.

A bull gorilla stood there, barely twenty feet away, glaring at them. It was a magnificent specimen, over seven feet tall and with a glossy black coat. Over its shoulders, like a mantle, was a silvery-gray sheen of hair. A silverback! Deep-set red eyes watched them carefully. One huge paw gripped a tree branch, the other, as thick as a weight-lifter's thigh, rested on the ground.

"Strewth!" Wallace gasped. It was one thing to see a gorilla in a cage at a zoo, listless and bored, but to meet one at large . . .

"Don't move!" Cathy hissed, for him and for the other policemen. They had fallen silent, watching the huge beast. "You may scare it."

"Scare *it*?" Wallace muttered.

The immense anthropoid suddenly raised its fists and thrummed its chest, howling loudly, huge, slavering fangs exposed. Everyone but Cathy moved back involuntarily.

"It's a ritual gesture of challenge," Cathy said softly. "It won't attack as long as we don't look aggressive."

"No fear of that," one of the policemen said weakly.

Despite what Cathy had said, the gorilla took a step forward, hammering on its chest again, repeating the scream of defiance. Then it started a rolling dash for them.

Cathy remained perfectly still, but not the policemen with rifles. Dropping to their knees, they swung their weapons up to their chests and fired almost in unison.

Cathy yelled out in wordless fury, expecting the gorilla's chest to burst into blood and shattered flesh. Instead, the gorilla barely paused, shook itself, and continued to charge.

Whipping up her own rifle, Cathy fired, then reloaded and fired again. Both shots hit the enraged beast high in the chest. The terrified policemen scattered, but Cathy stood her ground, waiting for the drug to take effect. Both darts had hit the beast—then why was it still moving?

It was as though the next seconds happened in slow motion, events almost frozen in time. Cathy could see, very clearly, where her two darts had fallen to the forest floor. She could see the shafts of sunlight lancing through the leaves of the trees, reflecting from the gorilla's coat. She could hear the enraged ape screaming, and then saw one huge paw swinging toward her, a blow powerful enough to crack her skull like an eggshell.

She rolled with the blow, flinging herself backward a second before the giant fist connected. It didn't completely miss her, and pain exploded through her neck and left shoulder as she spun backward and fell to the ground. Then the gorilla was past her and gone.

Dazed, without the strength to move, she lay on her back staring up at the sky. Her shoulder felt like it was broken, which was at least a good sign—it meant that she wasn't dead. Her vision was all fuzzy, and the sky refused to stay still. Finally, a blurred shape bent over her and someone grabbed her left wrist, feeling for a pulse. She screamed, terrible pain shooting up her arm.

"Sorry, ma'am," a voice apologized. "Think you can sit up?"

"I'll try." Her voice sounded choked and far off, but at least the words emerged from her mouth. With the gentle aid of the constable, she struggled to sit up. When the spinning in her head stopped, she could make out Wallace, checking two fallen policemen twenty feet away. The officer helping her followed her gaze.

"The two marksmen. It tossed them both aside like they was rag dolls," he said, his voice a mixture of fear and awe. "Then it vanished into the trees. Thank God. We need more men to deal with that . . . monster."

"You need more than men," Cathy told him. She was finally coming back to her senses, and she managed to scramble to her feet. After a dizzying moment, the world settled down and behaved itself. "I'd suggest a bazooka, or a medium-sized tank. Professionally speaking, of course." She managed to flex the fingers of her left arm. It hurt, but at least she'd not broken anything. The judo training had paid off there.

Wallace stumbled back to her, looking ashen. "Both dead," he told her, looking like he wanted to throw up. "God, that thing was strong."

"It was more than strong," she told him. "It was *wrong*."

"What?" Wallace pulled himself together with an effort. "What are you talking about?"

She led him across to where her two darts had fallen. Picking up the first, she thrust it under his nose. "I hit it with two of these," she told him. "They would have stopped a bull elephant mid-charge."

Wallace examined the dart. The needle was bent out of shape, as though it had struck something impenetrable. "I don't understand."

Disgusted, Cathy led him to where the ape had been standing when the dead marksmen had fired at it. "That thing bent my hypodermics, took two bullets in the chest, and shrugged them off like flies. That means one of two things. It was either wearing a bulletproof vest, or . . ." She bent down and grabbed a handful from the ground. It was a mat of fur, which she waved at Wallace. "Or it isn't really a gorilla at all."

"But we saw it!" Wallace exclaimed.

"We saw *something*," was all that Cathy would concede.

"Then if it wasn't a gorilla, what was it?"

Cathy opened her hand and looked down at the piece of fur. It was obviously synthetic, and designed to cover the—well, whatever it was. She turned the fur over in her hand. In faint letters on the back were the words *Knight Industries*. "I don't know yet," she said firmly. "But I intend to find out."

7 In Which Steed Calls on an Old Friend—And Emma Hears Voices

If there was one thing in the world that Edwin Carruthers, late of Cambridge University, could appreciate, it was a beautiful machine. Carruthers had been in love with physics almost as soon as he could walk. According to legend, Newton had required an apple to discover the law of gravity; Carruthers had deduced the facts from tossing a rattle out of his crib when still less than a year old. Einstein's theories of relativity were idle breakfast chatter before Carruthers reached his teens. People and their petty, unscientific ways did not interest him at all. But the machine . . .

The glories of a machine designed to utter perfection! The fluid grace of levers and joints, of connections and command, of the subjection of form to function. He was admiring a particularly fine specimen of the human machine when he was rather rudely brought back to the dull, senseless world of the human being.

"Er, I'm sorry . . ." he stammered, pushing the spectacles back up to the bridge of his nose. (He didn't need them—the lenses were simply panes of glass—but found them useful when intimidating the unscientific.) "What did you say?"

"I said," the wonderfully functional machine repeated, "that you aren't paying me the slightest attention, Carruthers." Mrs. Emma Peel smiled, a catlike grin that lent her blue-green eyes more than a touch of mystique. "It appears that I was entirely correct."

Carruthers blushed, and forced his purely scientific appreciation of her wonderful limbs into the back of his mind. It didn't like being relegated to his subconscious, and expressed its dislike by surfacing from time to time to embarrass him further. She was so amazingly built, and fitted perfectly into the dark blue cat suit . . .

Emma leaned forward and Carruthers swallowed, trying not to follow the contours of her body. Instead, he concentrated on the small pile of papers that she pushed over toward him. "There's a mistake somewhere in your calculations," she repeated.

"What?" That accusation was the only one that could ever really hurt him; he had not made an error in any of his mathematics since he reached the age of three. "Impossible."

"Then something's wrong," she insisted. "Your automation of the three factories that I reluctantly allowed you to undertake has been disastrous. A twenty-four-percent *increase* in productivity was your forecast. We have instead been faced with a *loss* of eight percent."

"My figures are correct!" he insisted. "There has to be an error introduced in areas over which I have no control."

"Really?" Emma arched an eyebrow to show her skepticism. "Do you perhaps think that the missing thirty-odd percent of production is caused by pilfering?" She pointed a finger down at the papers before them. "Workers would have to be smuggling complete battleships out under their hats to account for these errors!"

Drawing all his dignity about him (and trying to ignore how attractive she looked when she was angry), Carruthers replied: "Nevertheless, there has to be some exterior factor at work here, something that I have not been informed about."

Emma sighed and stood up. She had once reveled in the challenges offered by industry. Knight Industries had been founded by her father thirty years before, and with his death, she had taken over the running of the company. She had a flair for the work, but there were times when it seemed less than invigorating. On such days she almost wished that—She quenched *that* thought instantly. She was certain that she didn't want those days back again.

Did she?

She put an arm about Carruthers's shoulders, totally oblivious of the effect that she was having on the middle-aged scientist. Her desk was dwarfed in the office by the huge computer that ran down the outside wall. It was a state-of-the-art model, costing almost a hundred thousand pounds, with several thousand bytes of memory. The three factories that Carruthers had worked on automating fed their data directly into this machine.

"On your advice," she purred softly, "I purchased and installed this computer. I allowed you the freedom to program and operate it. It predicted the growth patterns for you; for me, it produces an eight-percent loss. Explanation, please?"

"It is a machine, Mrs. Peel," Carruthers protested. "It feeds out only what is fed into it. If you do not feed into it the right information, naturally you get back wrong results." He toyed with his glasses again. "Computers *are* the wave of the future," he said, warming to his subject. "Why, I believe that in fifty years there will be computers small enough to . . ." He looked around for inspiration. "To sit on the corner of your desk!" he exclaimed wildly. "Computers that will be smarter and faster than the one we have here."

Emma had to smile at his enthusiasm. "Fifty years?" she echoed. "That long? Surely, twenty years at the most. Science is advancing faster than many of us think." She could recall a few brushes of her own with scientific experiments that were far ahead of their time.

"Fifty years, twenty, whatever," Carruthers conceded. "The point is that no matter how advanced a system is, its output will still depend on what is fed into it." He marched to the computer and started fingering the large keyboard. "If what is fed in is not perfectly correct, then how can it be expected to . . ." His voice trailed off as the printer started to chatter. Bemused, he stared at the machine; he had not ordered it to print anything. As soon as it had finished hammering away, he tore out the page of paper. He stared at it, but it made no sense.

"What is it," Emma asked, moving lithely to join him.

"I don't understand it," he sniffed, handing her the sheet. "Does this mean anything to you?"

She took the paper and smoothed it out on her desktop. There were exactly four words printed on it:

MRS. PEEL, YOU'RE NEEDED

"No, Steed!" she yelled into the air. "Not now!"

"And I'm delighted to see you again, too, Mrs. Peel."

Carruthers spun around, not having heard anyone enter the room. In the doorway, leaning nonchalantly on an umbrella, stood a man dressed impeccably in gray, with a jaunty bowler tipped to one side and a broad grin lighting his handsome face. The newcomer bore an incredible likeness to the man in the photograph sitting on Mrs. Peel's desk. "Your husband?" Carruthers asked, embarrassed once again by his thoughts about Mrs. Peel.

"No," said Emma without turning around. "*His* name is Steed. Say good-bye to him."

"Oh, don't send him out on my account." Steed grinned, striding over to join them. "But I would like a word or two."

Emma spun around and glared at Steed. "I don't believe it," she snapped (the first time Carruthers had ever seen her completely lose her composure). "You just stride in here and expect me to drop everything and follow you off to—to—to who-knows-where, just like that? Really, Steed!"

"Come at a bad time, have I?" Steed asked sympathetically. Using the ferrule of his umbrella, he poked at the papers that Carruthers had left on the desk. "Profits down, company crisis, that sort of thing?" She could tell he was genuinely pleased to see her, despite her less than cordial welcome; his face never lost the cheery smile.

"Steed, this might just be a game to you," Emma said coldly, "but to me, it's my career, my lasting achievement, my—"

"I get the picture," he said breezily. "And because I care, I'll help you. Then you can help me."

Over the years that she had worked with Steed, Emma had heard a lot from him, but this last comment simply took her breath away. All she could do was stare at him and marvel at his unbounded cheek.

Less wise, Carruthers continued the conversation. "You are an expert in business?"

"No," Steed admitted honestly.

"In computers, then?"

"Far from it."

Frowning, Carruthers had to push at his glasses again. "Then how do you expect to help?"

"Because there is one thing I am an expert in," Steed smiled. "And it will help you immensely."

"Sipping champagne, Steed? There's no bubbly here," Emma interjected dryly.

The line of Steed's jaw hardened. "Really? That's too bad. However, I meant my *other* speciality."

"And that would be?" she prompted.

"Lying." Steed smiled, a twinkle in his eye. Turning back to Carruthers, he explained: "False information needn't simply be information omitted; surely there's the possibility that someone is deliberately feeding the computer false information?"

Carruthers blinked. "You mean . . . that someone has introduced a deliberate flaw into my machine?"

"I think you've got it!" Steed exclaimed. "Now, why not run along and check it out. Mrs. Peel and I have some other business to discuss."

Scooping up the printouts, Carruthers did literally run out, enthused with a fresh theory to check. Steed politely waited for the door to slam before turning back to Mrs. Peel.

"I don't believe it," she stormed, stomping back behind her desk. "How could you just walk in here and—and—"

"I know," Steed said softly. "I read about Peter's death, and I'm very sorry. I wouldn't have come to you at all if there had been anyone else. I need someone I can trust."

Emma paused, her anger evaporating. Steed's habitual good-natured charm seemed brittle, in danger of snapping. She had seen him in many moods, but this one was new to her. She *knew* why he had never attended Peter's funeral, why he had not made an appearance when she had needed him most. If he had come to her then, he might never have found the strength to leave again.

A look of concern crossed her face. "Tara?" she asked.

"Compromised." He frowned. "And I don't want to place her in further danger."

"But you'll place me in danger?"

"Never that, Mrs. Peel. If I thought it would do that, I wouldn't be here." From his pocket, Steed produced the tape he had taken from Charles. "It's your scientific expertise I'm after."

"You say the sweetest things, Steed." But she smiled as she said it. There was no need for words now. Both of them knew what they would have liked to say, but both knew they would never admit the truth to one another. Steed's chosen profession allowed him no serious entanglements; he had to be ready to be sent anywhere at a moment's notice. A passing romance was one thing, a casual flirting with some diverting member of the opposite sex; Steed was very good at that. But he could never allow his true feelings for her to show through. He was on the firing line every day of his life; a wife would have left him open to the opposition, or to be killed. She shuddered, and suppressed her thoughts.

"It's a gift," he replied, handing her the tape.

Emma nodded and walked to her desk. Pulling open the top drawer revealed a compact tape deck. Silently she threaded the spool Steed had given her onto the blank reel and turned on the machine. When the message had ended, she reached slowly forward and clicked off the machine.

"Mother?" she scoffed. "Killing someone?" She stared at him, waiting for his reply.

"One of *us*. An agent named Keller. You never met him."

Emma shook her head. "That's not the sort of thing one expects from one's Mother."

"That's not what they think at the Ministry."

"*Think?*" she asked. "Or are *afraid of?*"

"The latter, I'd say." Steed sat down and put his feet up on her desk. She stared at him but said nothing. The look on his face said it all; Steed was a worried man—a very worried man, if she read his behavior correctly. He glanced at the picture of Emma's dead husband. "I really am sorry."

She could follow his gaze. "I know. You were saying?"

His work had to come first. "We know from experience that there are always a few bad apples in any espionage group, but the idea that Mother might have gone over has sent shock waves through the Department. They even called Charles back out of retirement to handle the affair." He sighed. "He's ordered me to eliminate Mother."

"What?" Emma couldn't believe it. She'd seen Steed kill in the past—more than once—and do it without regret. But he had never deliberately set out to kill, to the best of her knowledge. The thought of Steed becoming an assassin, even for the Department, was unthinkable. "Isn't that a little out of your line?"

"Totally," he admitted frankly. "So Charles must have given me the assignment for that very reason. I'm the one agent he could trust not to go out and bump off dear old Mother simply because I'd been ordered to."

"Charles believes Mother to be innocent?"

"Precisely. I *know* that Mother is not a killer, or a traitor, and I'm sure you agree. So there has to be some other explanation."

Emma removed the tape from the machine. "It's too good a recording to be a mimic," she said.

"Naturally; if it hadn't been good, we'd never have been allowed to tape it. To swallow the bait, Mrs. Peel. Which leaves . . . ?"

"Electronics," she confirmed. "Some kind of voice synthesizer, probably. Let's visit the laboratory."

The room to which she led Steed was one of several in the complex of buildings that made up the London headquarters of Knight Industries. The firm had long been known for innovative research, and under Emma's control it had been even more successful. Her insistence on funding pure research had taken many knocks at shareholders' meetings, but she refused to back down on her belief that it was the only way to prepare for the future. She could see too many British companies losing out to foreign competitors because of their lack of ability and unwillingness to change. Naturally, she never revealed that many of her insights had come from missions with Steed. They had fought many crazed scientists together, and Emma's retentive mind had kept on file anything that might someday be of use. Now, back at the helm of Knight Industries, she could apply those lessons. She pushed a metal door open and ushered Steed inside.

"Impressive," Steed said, looking around the well-stocked room. He had very little interest in science himself, and wouldn't have been able to tell a voltmeter from a vacuum tube. Emma knew this, and ignored his feigned enthusiasm.

Leading the way to a low workbench halfway down the room, she began to power up the units that were built into the woodwork. It seemed to be a tape deck with a number of cathode-ray tubes connected to it. Two rows of control levers and knobs were laid into the panel on which she worked to get the equipment ready. "This is a sonic analyzer," she explained, seeing the questioning look on Steed's face.

"Does it fry chips?" he asked.

"It helps in our work on low-frequency sound and its effects on metal." A flicker of a smile crossed her lips as she hooked the device to a bank of four monitor screens. "We needed some sensitive methods of taking apart the components of sound."

"Every home should have one," Steed murmured. "You mean that if I played a Beatles record into this, all of the gadgetry here could break the song down into its component parts?"

"Something like that."

"Wonderful. I like this thing already." Steed was a traditionalist in his musical tastes. He preferred a brass band or a full orchestra any day over four long-haired young men yelling over electronic noise. His only relief was the conviction that the musical insanity known as rock and roll would never last.

Emma ignored his remark and fed the machine the tape Steed had brought. Then she pointed to the bank of monitors. "Keep your eyes on those, Steed." She started up the tape, and they listened to Mother's voice once again. With each word, the screens lit up. Oscilloscopic traces wiggled luminously across them. Emma waited a moment and froze the pictures.

Steed peered at the first and grinned. "I once

dated a girl with a face like that—as a favor to my Aunt Millicent."

Emma ignored his remark. "These are the various components of the taped message," she said. "The second screen shows a background hum that's consistent with that produced by telephone-tapping machines. Obviously the recorder that made this tape, so we can eliminate that." Shutting down this monitor, she indicated the next. "Screen three shows the background noise of the open telephone line, so that one goes."

"Leaving us with Aunt Millie," said Steed. He tapped the first screen with his umbrella. "All those horrible peaks and valleys—it reminds me of my days on the Matterhorn."

"You never told me that you'd climbed the Matterhorn, Steed."

"Never did," he replied blandly. "Spent my time in this charming little inn, tucked away in the mountains. Let the rest of the team tackle the slope while I tackled some excellent Beaujolais."

Emma fixed him with a steely glare. "This pattern is the voice code of Mother." She indicated the screen.

Eyeing the trace critically, Steed couldn't resist adding: "Looks like he needs a tonsillectomy."

"*This* one," Emma sighed, tapping the fourth screen, "is the interesting one. The pattern is faint, but it's there."

"So it is," Steed agreed, looking at the mass of wavering lines. "But what is it?"

"I'd say the hum of the machine being used to synthesize Mother's voice. Inaudible to the human ear, of course, but this equipment can pick it out.

It's almost a perfect copy of the real thing."

"But only almost. Bravo, Mrs. Peel. I knew you'd find it."

Shutting down the equipment, Emma sat and looked up at him. "And now that I've found it?"

He smiled, the old devil-may-care grin that she remembered from so many escapades together. "Now I go and have a chat with Mother. He'll be most interested to hear our story. Can you spare the time to join me? I'll need you to explain all this technical mumbo-jumbo."

As Emma was about to reply, the door burst open and Carruthers raced in, skidding to a halt at her side. "There you are, there you are!" he exclaimed, waving a sheaf of papers under Steed's nose. "You were right, Mr. Steed—someone has been *lying* to my computer. Lying! No wonder the poor dear coughed up a load of nonsense." He seemed shocked at the concept. One clearly did not do such things.

"And?" Emma prompted.

"It's the factory just outside of Crawley," he answered excitedly, scrabbling at the papers. "Their figures have been falsified. The other two factories are producing genuine data—but the Crawley computer is making false claims!"

Emma nodded, but privately she had problems understanding why an entire factory would falsify its output records. Surely whoever was behind the deception would have to know he'd be caught sooner or later? And where was the purloined material going? She had a horrible suspicion that perhaps Steed had arrived at exactly the right time. For all his idiosyncrasies, he was excellent at solving problems, and one of the few people in the world she trusted implicitly to back her up when trouble threatened. "Steed—" she began, but he cut her short.

"Of course, Mrs. Peel," he said, reading her thoughts. "Mother first, then we'll look into this computer business. Haven't been to Crawley in years." He smiled fondly. "There used to be this wonderful little country pub there, served the best mutton sandwiches—and a good, strong pint of ale."

Emma rose to her feet without thinking. It was less than a year since she had sworn that this would never, never happen again. But Steed needed help, and . . . well, life had been rather boring of late. . . .

Left alone in the laboratory, Carruthers began to gather up his papers, a puzzled look on his face. "The strangest time to visit that chap's mother," he muttered to himself. He shook his head and scurried off to do further analysis.

8 Tara Finds Her V.O.I.C.E.

Tara glanced at the sign on the gate, shrugged to herself, and then drove into the grounds of the small country mansion. The sign had proclaimed: V.O.I.C.E.; Tara hoped it would speak words of wisdom.

One of the things she loved most about England was its ability to breed those gloriously eccentric souls that the rest of the world looked upon as being typically British: people with a deep, abiding love of—nay, devotion to—a cause or concept that the majority of the population scorned or ignored. English eccentrics abounded, and she had learned from her association with Steed that the word "eccentric" didn't automatically mean "wrong." Many personages who were undeniably eccentric still had their roots firmly planted in reality; it was simply their aspirations and ideals that surmounted the clouds of the mundane. Perhaps on topics outside of their speciality they were hopelessly lost, but when it came to their area of expertise . . .

Stopping her car in the driveway outside the manor house, she noted with amusement the small van parked there. It had a loudspeaker funnel mounted on its roof, and its sides were adorned with a painting of a stylized open mouth—complete with tonsils—enclosing the letters V.O.I.C.E. The same emblem was proudly blazoned across the huge front doors. She climbed the steps and pressed the large red button on the tip of the tongue—presumably the doorbell.

A loud, resonating voice called out: "Visitors!" Accompanied by a loud banging sound, the door jerked open.

"Yes?"

For a moment, Tara was taken aback. The man who had answered the door was definitely on the bizarre side. He was tall, thin, and stooped. Skin and a very meager layer of flesh clothed his bones. His attire hung loosely from his frame, so he resembled nothing more than a skeleton hastily stuffed into whatever odd collection of garments were at hand. He wore unmatched socks—one red, one green-and-blue striped. His trousers were black, held up by a thick yellow belt. His shirt had begun life (presumably) as white, but had so many breakfast stains dabbed across it that it was difficult to be certain. His half-knotted tie—twisted askew to the left—was an old school memento; it looked as if the old school had collapsed upon it and the tie had then been wrenched out from underneath the bricks. The apparition's white hair stuck out over his ears in a tangle, and the top of his bald skull was brightly polished. A pair of rimless spectacles perched atop this dome completed the picture.

"Yes?" he squawked again.

Tara managed to find her voice at last. "Hello. I have a problem, and was told that V.O.I.C.E. could help."

"Then don't stand there dithering," the creature said, grabbing her with a bony arm. "Come in, come in."

Steering Tara into the mansion, he led her across a small hall and then into a large, wood-lined room. The walls, roof, and floor were all of polished ash, as were the table, chairs, and bookshelves. The latter were filled to overflowing with an astounding number of books. Charts were tacked up on the walls, demonstrating such matters as phonetic punctuation, various language equivalents, and the shapes of the mouth when making certain sounds.

"Well," said the figure brusquely, "say what's on your mind. Or, as we like to say here"—he wheezed at his own joke—"do find your voice!"

Tara stared around in fascination. There were books on every language she had ever heard of, and several she hadn't. There were charts of pronunciation, and others on throat and larynx diseases. There were magazines dealing with communications and translation. "A veritable Tower of Babel," she remarked, without stopping to think.

"Babel?" her host snapped. "*Babel?* Certainly not, young lady! At Babel, all languages were confounded, you know. Here, *here*"—he waved all about himself expansively—"they are made clear. That is the nature of V.O.I.C.E.!"

"What is?" Tara asked, fascinated despite herself.

"Don't you know about us?" He seemed surprised.

Tara shook her head. "Well, no. I was referred to you by a friend. I have a problem—"

"So you said; no need to repeat yourself!" The man tucked his hands into his pockets and drew himself to his full height—an impressive six feet, four inches. "Then welcome to V.O.I.C.E.—the Venerable Order of Inter-Communicative Endeavors!"

"I beg your pardon?"

"Statements said once do not need repeating!" her host snapped primly. "Kindly pay attention! What is the merit of communication if only one of us is listening, eh? Tell me that!" He gave her no chance to reply, but instead stuck out one bony finger and waved it in her direction. "What is the primary difference between men and apes?"

"Men shave more frequently?" Tara suggested teasingly.

The man's face cracked into a small smile. "Jocularity!" he exclaimed. "Excellent! Quite correct! The difference between men and apes—between men and all other creatures upon this Earth—is the human ability to communicate. Human beings are characterized by their desire, their willingness, their *imperative* to communicate with others of their species! We speak in words—thousands, millions, quadrillions of words! Whatever you want to describe—why, be sure the Greeks had a word for it. Did you know that Eskimos have seventeen words for 'snow'? That the first artificial language was created by the Polish Dr. Zamenhof in 1887 and named 'Esperanto'—his own word for hope? He foresaw a universal language as the hope for mankind! Why, human beings have a positive genius for communication that passes beyond mere words. For two lovers, a sigh and the moon in the sky can be enough to speak volumes even the greatest poets could never transcribe! In short, it is the human genius at communication that we at V.O.I.C.E. celebrate—nay, glorify!"

As the man took a breath, Tara launched in with: "You didn't mention your name."

"Didn't I?" he exclaimed. "How terribly remiss of me. Lipp. With two P's." He stuck out a bony hand and shook hers. "Professor Isaiah Lipp, at your service. Delighted to meet you, Miss . . . ah?"

"King," she replied. "Tara King."

"Tara?" he echoed. "What a glorious name! Tara—the home of the Sidhe, the faerie folk of Ireland! The dwelling place of the mystical and fantastic! The embodiment of mystery and awe!"

"Actually," she told him in apology, "I was named from my mother's favorite film—*Gone With The Wind*."

"Another example of the human ability to communicate," Lipp said, completely unabashed. "The cinematic glories! The visual delights—"

"Professor," she broke in, politely but firmly. "My problem?"

"What? Oh, yes." Lipp ground to a halt for a moment and then nodded. "Excuse me, please, my dear. I do tend to get a trifle carried away when I have visitors. It's a perfectly normal human urge to communicate, but I admit that I do at times take it somewhat to an extreme. I forget that my guests also desire a little rapport. Pray continue, and I shall pay the most avid attention."

Removing the tape she had taken from Mother from her voluminous handbag, Tara handed it to her host. "This tape was ostensibly made by a colleague of mine," she explained. "But I suspect that it's a fake."

"Ah!" Lipp leaped out of his chair and clutched the recording. "A challenge, eh? To see if this is a genuine voice or a spurious one!" He grinned at her, enhancing his likeness to a skull. "Well, they'll have to get up very early in the morning to fool Isaiah Lipp, believe you me! Follow me, Miss King!"

He led her into an adjoining room, this one filled with speakers spread across the entire length of the rear wall. Some were only inches across, but four of them were no less than six feet in width. It looked like a stereo expert's dream of heaven. The other three walls were covered in thick acoustic tiles. Positioned by the wall directly opposite the speakers stood a small raised console. As Lipp led his way there, he called over his shoulder: "Close the door, my dear! Acoustics! Acoustics! This room is designed to give perfect playback, no matter what the weaknesses of the source material. But it cannot do that if extrinsic sounds are allowed to creep into the room."

Doing as she had been bidden, Tara then joined him at the console. He fed the tape into a small deck set into the machinery. Carefully, he set a whole bank of volume and tone controls to level number two, then grinned at her.

"It wouldn't do to listen to it any louder," he confessed. "This room is acoustically perfect. Too high a volume would distort the result." With a wave of his hand, he proudly indicated the speaker cabinets. "Those are arranged so that each one cancels the weaknesses of its neighbor. What we shall hear is the perfectly undistorted quality of the recording you have brought."

With a flourish, he started the tape. Seconds later, Steed's voice flooded the room. Tara winced at the volume, but Lipp seemed completely unaffected.

"I see what you mean," she said. "It's rather loud."

"Loud?" he scoffed. "Nonsense, dear child—I have this deck on one of the lowest settings. If I were to make it *loud*, then you'd really hear something. Before your eardrums ruptured," he added cheerfully.

Tara could believe him. Even at this "low" setting, she could feel a slight vibration buzzing in her ears.

As suddenly as it began, the tape ended and Lipp turned off the machine. "Good," he informed her. "Very good indeed."

Tara had heard nothing apart from Steed's voice. "But?" she prompted.

"Oh, but not *perfect*." He grinned again and explained, "To a novice in the science of acoustics, such as yourself, it sounds like a human voice. But to trained ears like mine, it's—"

"A fake?" Tara suggested.

"It's a very sophisticated form of voice replicator, my dear. You understand the principle?" The expression on Tara's face answered his question. "Electronic circuits can be made to produce any sound. With sufficient sophistication and patience, you can use such circuits to reproduce any natural sound. There are a few such devices currently available, Miss King. And certainly not many as sophisticated as the machine that made that recording. I suspect that we have a genius at work! Such refinement, such clarity of composition, such precision of tone! The sort of thing, in fact . . ." His voice trailed away as he was struck by a sudden thought. "It sounds *precisely* like the sort of thing my own invention would produce."

"*Your* invention?"

"Yes." Lipp was clearly very puzzled. "As I said earlier, the main point that differentiates the human from the animal is the ability to communicate. I have always felt sorrow for those poor people who are unable to vocalize. Those who were struck dumb at birth, or lost the capacity to speak through some capricious accident. For some years now, I have been working on a voice synthesizer that would be small enough to carry around on one's person—a portable model. So they can use it to communicate with others."

Tara could feel her feminine intuition kicking into high gear. "Were those experiments a success?"

"Yes," said Lipp absentmindedly. "But there was not enough interest in the phonetic joys to allow me to work independently. My meager resources were soon used up. To enable me to complete my work on the device, I was forced to take in a partner."

"You completed your work?" Tara's brain was working overtime. "Did you produce such a machine?"

"Oh, yes, of course. Over here." He led the way to the far end of the room, by the speakers, then inserted a key into a barely visible lock concealed in one of the acoustic tiles. From the well-concealed cupboard he took a small package, attached to a miniature keyboard. It was similar in appearance to the main console, though much smaller. A series of dials covered the front panel. "Each key is a single phoneme," he explained, "a phoneme being the basic unit of sound." He pressed the first key and the box made the noise: "*Aaaay.*"

"Using the dials, you can alter the tone," Lipp explained. "Instill it with a little more personality, so to speak. I do so hate those machines that can only produce reedy noises that grate on one's ears."

Tara was thinking on a different level. "Or you could use that machine, set correctly, to duplicate a real person's voice?"

"Well, yes," Lipp agreed reluctantly. "Though that was never my intention. A person's voice is so utterly unique, so completely individual. To reproduce such natural perfection would be somewhat akin to rape." He blinked. "Pardon me, my dear, but I'm sure you understand that I feel very strongly indeed about such an appalling idea."

"Perhaps it was not *your* aim," she told him. "But if there is someone else who knows about the synthesizer . . . Professor, does someone else have a device like this?"

"Certainly not, Miss King. Not even my backer from Knight Industries—"

"Tut, tut, Isaiah," said a soft voice from the doorway. "How trusting we are. Of course I have a device. It's proving to be most useful." Tara and Lipp spun around to face the intruder. He held a gun, aimed steadily in their direction. Tara checked her impulse to move.

"Admirable self-control, Miss King," the man told her. He was bundled up in a raincoat, with a hat pulled down over his eyes. His hands were gloved, and little of his face could be seen. He looked short and thick-set, but she couldn't tell if that was natural or merely on account of the bulky clothing he wore.

"Professor," the man said regretfully, "it's quite apparent that I cannot trust you to keep what you know to yourself. But that is what happens, I suspect, when one deals with a man so committed to communication. The concept of discretion seems to have passed you by. Your urge to communicate will prove very costly—for you."

"You deceived me!" Lipp yelled, pointing his bony finger at the intruder. "*You* were responsible for that tape. Merciful heavens, I actually listened to the sound of a man being murdered! I shall never be a party to such a knavish action, and will expose you for all the world to know as a killer and a fraud!"

The figure in the doorway sighed. "I was afraid you'd take it like that, Professor." He crossed to the console and started to adjust the settings, with obvious expertise. The gun, still covering them, never wavered. "So I'm afraid that I must, ah, still your voice rather permanently. Miss King, you have my apologies—your demise was not supposed to happen quite this soon. But the best-laid plans and all of that . . ." He finished his manipulations, then used the gun butt to smash the controls, locking them into place. Finally, he started the speakers to life and jammed the last control.

Behind them, the wall of speakers began to play Ravel's "Bolero." It started softly—a mere deafening level. Tara could feel her bones shaking with the incredible decibels she was being exposed to—in the quiet section.

The man at the console laughed and saluted them mockingly with his gun before dashing out the door and closing it behind him. Tara could hear none of this, as the music drowned out everything. She ran to the door and tried to open it, but found it locked. Nothing she did would budge it.

The sound was building. It was like a physical thing, already hammering at her body. How long before the noise became too terrible to bear? She couldn't recall the piece well enough to know how long the quiet section lasted. She knew that the intensity would build up, and up—and that the level of sound would probably shake them to death. It was of little consolation to know that her eardrums would probably burst before then, rendering her deaf to the murderous noise.

She staggered over to the console, the music howling through her mind. Lipp had already reached it and was frantically trying to get it to function. But the would-be killer had done too effective a job. Lipp caught her questioning look and shook his head. There was nothing to be done here. He reached for his glasses, but the lenses shattered into countless fragments. The sound of that explosion was lost in the general roar.

As the music swelled, Tara's head felt like it was being attacked with jackhammers, boring through the bone into her brain. Clutching her ears did no good at all. Frantically she tore strips off her blouse and tried to stuff them into her ears, to no real effect. Lipp shook his head again. Diving into a pocket, he pulled out a battered notepad and pencil, then scrawled away.

Looking over his shoulder, Tara read: "No good—it's the vibrations that will kill us—shake us apart."

She could feel what he meant. Even though it was the noise level that was staggering, there was a level of vibration that set her teeth on edge and made her bones ache. As the sound intensity rose, the vibration would get worse and worse, until it literally shook them apart.

A sudden idea hit her, and she grabbed the pad and pencil. "Your portable voice generator," she wrote hastily. "Convert it to higher-than-top-C and use it on the lock."

Lipp had to squint without the aid of his glasses to read her note, and nodded as he caught her idea. He staggered across the room, fighting against the increased sound until he had reached the discarded equipment. Picking it up, he clutched it to his chest and ran back to join her at the door.

They both settled down by the locked door, trying to shield themselves as best they could. The music was pounding almost physically at them, rocking them from side to side with the rhythmic pulses. Lipp feverishly worked to set the synthesizer, then twisted the frequency dial as far to the right as it would go. He placed the small speaker against the door lock and turned the machine on.

It was impossible for her ears to make out the additional noise—which was probably outside the audible range, anyway—but Tara could see the effects of what the synthesizer was doing. The door began to shake, and then it simply gave way.

Grabbing the professor, she dragged him outside. Even in the corridor, the sound was staggeringly loud. Lipp was obviously on the verge of collapse, but he retained the strength to shut down the synthesizer. Tara managed to get him outdoors, where the strains of "Bolero" were merely incredibly loud.

As she collapsed onto the grass, Lipp fell over beside her, mercifully unconscious. Hearing the sound of exploding glass, Tara glanced back. The house was shaking with the vibrations, and even as she watched, the bricks and mortar started to crack. The house was literally shaking itself apart. The roof tiles looked as though they were dancing, and the windows had bowed out and shattered. Then the house began to collapse inward. The walls rocked, rolled, and then caved in. Though this must have resulted in a great deal of noise, she could hear nothing over the music.

Then, abruptly, the music stopped as the power lines were severed by falling masonry. In what would otherwise have been blessed silence, the entire building slammed in on itself, dust and bricks spraying out. Finally there was no sound at all. All that was left of the house was a pile of broken roof rafters, bricks, and dust.

Spotting the synthesizer still clutched in Lipp's

fingers, Tara eased it from his grasp, giving it a big hug. It was so hard to judge which was the more wonderful—to be alive, or to be in blessed silence.

In the trees, a chorus of birds started to sing, but Tara could barely hear anything now. She staggered back to her feet. Lipp would recover soon enough, but she had no time to wait around and thank him. She recalled their assailant's words, that *she* was meant to die later. He obviously knew what she was up to, and it seemed clear that he had to have Steed targeted as well. At least she was a step closer to uncovering the man behind the plot: she now knew that he worked for a firm called Knight Industries. That could come later, though—first of all, she had to find Steed and warn him.

She ran to her car and started it. She could barely hear the ignition; she frowned, hoping her hearing would return soon. Throwing the car into gear, she raced away, heading back toward London.

If Steed had believed Brodny's report, he would have driven to Henley. As soon as he discovered that the Russian was wrong, he'd probably head back to his apartment. Tara decided to head there first, since it was on the way, on the off chance that he'd be there, or at least had left some kind of note for her to find.

She could only hope that she'd reach him before the unknown opposition did.

9 Ale and Farewell

Cathy stopped her car and looked about her. She was barely a hundred yards south of Oxford Street, but the shoppers who scurried with their packages and frozen smiles along that thoroughfare rarely ventured into Soho. The district had once been the domain of the fruit sellers, purveying their goods from handcarts. Within the space of six months, the food traders had disappeared and the pushers of pornography had moved in. Berwick Street had become the home of the seediest of "clubs," where men in dirty raincoats ogled naked women, who eked out a despairingly miserable existence as "hostesses."

The place was not considered a safe area for women to frequent—unless they were "performers" in one of the dingier theaters. The men who ventured into this section tended to regard women as mere sex objects, not thinking human beings who possessed any form of rights. Anyone who entertained such notions about Cathy, though, was quickly discouraged by the firm set of her jaw, the casual self-assurance in her stance, and the flicker of burning anger in her eyes.

It took her barely ten minutes to find the man she was seeking, propped up outside the back entrance of one of the worst dives in the area. A half-empty bottle of scotch lay cradled in one hand, while with the other he flicked the pages of a torn and discarded glossy magazine.

"Your reading tastes haven't improved, Charlie," she grunted.

Charlie—no one, especially himself, knew his last name; it had been washed away by alcohol years before Cathy had been born—looked up guiltily and slammed shut the skin rag. Since the cover was just as bad as the interior, he then stuffed it under the legs of his dirty, threadbare trousers. His unshaven, filthy face cracked into a gap-toothed smile. " 'Ello, Duchess," he croaked, sending whiskey-stained foul breath in her direction. "Long time no see."

Cathy wafted her hand in the air. "From the smell of things," she observed, "it's been a long time since you saw anything but pink elephants."

His whiskey-blurred eyes gazed down at the bottle in his arms. "Yeah, I knows what ya mean," he agreed. "I'm gonna give it up 'fore it kills me." After a pause, he added: "Or mebbe after." He scratched at the back of his head—probably dislodging a family of fleas in the process. "So, whatcha after, Duchess?"

"Information, Charlie." Despite his liquor-soaked brain, Charlie had a highly retentive memory, and he listened at a lot of doors that he shouldn't. He was one of the best stoolies Steed had ever discovered—and cultivated. Cathy suppressed a smile as she recalled the time that Steed had attempted to improve Charlie's insatiable thirst for whiskey. Instead of the scotch Charlie usually soaked himself in, Steed had donated a bottle of champagne. To Steed's horror, Charlie had chug-alugged the whole bottle in one breath. Thereafter, Steed had stuck to providing Charlie with his normal tipple. At least scotch lasted longer.

"It's a good day for that," Charlie replied, tapping the bottle he held. "Just had one consultation."

Somewhat reluctantly, Cathy fished a matching bottle from beneath her coat and passed it down to him. She hated adding to his drinking problem, but she knew from past experience that he would accept no other form of payment. Charlie looked at the label and snorted in appreciation. He slipped the bottle into a torn pocket of his filthy raincoat and looked up at her. "I likes to invest in me future," he said happily, patting his pocket. "So, what can I do to 'elp?"

"Knight Industries," she said. "What can you tell me?"

His eyes widened. "Odd," he replied. "That's what the last fella asked about."

Cathy's frown increased. "When?"

Charlie examined the level in his bottle. It was half gone. "Twenty minutes, tops," he told her. "Nice gent. Professional. Name of Keel."

"*David* Keel?"

Charlie shrugged. "Mebbe. Ain't on a first-name basis with me clients, Duchess." Such matters were of total indifference to him—as were bathing and other items of personal hygiene. "He knows Steed, though."

"And he was interested in Knight Industries?"

"Yeah." Charlie took a swig, then wiped his mouth on the back of his grubby hand. Cathy tried not to gag when he licked his fingers clean of whiskey. She hoped the alcohol had killed a few of the germs there. "He also asked about Marty Klein."

"There's a connection?"

"Yeah. Marty's a fist-for-'ire type, and 'e got a job a couple of days back for some bloke out at Knight in Crawley. Paid 'im well for puttin' the snatch on a doctor. Any'ow, turns out the doc was a friend of Keel's, and Keel ran into Marty's fist."

Cathy considered what she'd learned. It didn't seem to fit with a killer gorilla manufactured by the firm—but then again, nothing was right about this crazy setup. She knew that Keel had once worked with Steed, but where did the abduction of the doctor fit in? Perhaps a pooling of forces might pay off here . . . an exchange of information. "Do you know where Keel is?"

"Yeah, after Marty . . .'e's been free and easy with 'is money in 'is favorite pub. The 'Unting 'Orn, in Wexmouth Street."

Cathy nodded. "Thanks, Charlie. See you around."

Charlie managed a feeble salute. "Sure thing, Duchess. Any time." He raised the bottle. "I'll drink to that."

"You'll drink to anything, Charlie."

He smiled ingenuously. "Can I 'elp bein' an 'appy fella?"

"With that stuff in you? Not a chance."

The Hunting Horn was one of those family-type locals. Keel paused in the doorway, looking about the smoke-filled main bar. It held husbands who should have been at work, women who should have been minding the kids, and enough underage drinkers to get the owner of the place a long stay in a cell at the local police station. Most of the drinkers were smoking cigarettes, contributing to the stench in the air. A jukebox was trying to play Chuck Berry, but the noise of the conversations drowned most of it out. The stench of beer and sweaty bodies was overwhelming.

Crossing to the bar, Keel ordered a half of their best bitter ale. "Marty in tonight?" he asked, handing the barman his coins.

"Yeah." The man wasn't too interested. "He's in the lounge, in the snug by the window."

Thanking the man, Keel picked up his drink and passed through into the lounge bar, and into fresher air. Here were tables filled with empty glasses and packets of Smith's Crisps. Little blue papers that once held salt were scattered on the tabletops. There were only a dozen or so people in this room, and the level of noise was considerably lower.

Marty was sitting at the far end, instantly recognizable even without his mask. His bandaged hand and the hastily repaired tear in his jacket bore testimony to the bout of fisticuffs he had shared with Keel. Sitting with him was another unsavory-looking thug; Alfie, thought Keel.

A third man was playing darts. Retrieving the arrows from the dartboard, he sat down beside Marty and reached for a glass of beer. "Your turn, boss. Careful with that hand."

Grunting his disapproval of the man's joke, Marty gathered up the darts and stepped toward the board, taking liberal sips of ale as he considered his next throw. Keel sipped at his own ale, using the glass to shield his features from them when they glanced about indifferently to see who had come in. None of them paid him any further attention. Keel avoided bringing himself to their attention, and scanned the room, weighing up his chances of taking on Marty and his cronies in here.

There were two older men at one table, sitting with two old ladies in curlers and hair nets. Obviously pensioners, out for their midday constitutionals; they would not get involved in anything that might happen. One was crunching away at a packet of crisps—probably his idea of lunch—mechanically transferring them one at a time from the packet to his mouth. He had no teeth, and Keel suspected he was one of those people who had dentures and hated wearing them.

That left a group of six people at a table nearer to the smaller bar. They had the look of young toughs about them—leather jackets, slicked-back, Brylcreemed hair, and mean expressions. But were they with Marty? And even if not, would they decide to join in a free-for-all simply because they enjoyed mindless violence? It was impossible to tell.

Keel was in pretty good shape, despite the kick

that Marty had given him on leaving. The hospital had taped him up and advised him to avoid any strenuous exercise. The doctor would have a fit if he knew what Keel had planned. He had decided he needed an edge, somehow. He certainly didn't want to start trouble while any of the trio still held a dart in his hand. Suicide wasn't part of his plan.

He wandered outside and found the inspiration he was looking for. There was a black Ford parked in the back lot, by the outdoor toilets. It was the one he had caught a glimpse of when Marty and his boys had raided the house. Glancing around to make sure that there was no one in sight, he smashed the beer mug he held and went over to the car. With a wry grin, he slashed all four tires with the mug's jagged remains. Smiling as the air hissed out, he reentered the pub. In the smoke-filled main lounge, he managed to get the barman's attention.

"Know who owns the black Ford out back?" he yelled over the noise. "Some young punk just slashed all the tires on it."

"Bleedin' vandals," the man grunted. "It's Marty's—and he ain't gonna like that at all." He moved off to tell the bad news to Marty. Keel went back outside and waited in the shadows. After a moment, the back door opened and Marty, Alfie, and the third man came out.

"Bloomin' 'ell," Alfie snorted. "Look what they done to your car, Marty."

"I'm looking," Marty snarled furiously. "When I get my hands on the son of a bitch who did that, I'll—"

"You'll what?" Keel asked, moving in behind them.

The trio spun around. Keel saw their faces fall when they recognized him, and he enjoyed the sight.

"I see you've attempted to repair your jacket, Marty." Keel grinned. "You ought to get yourself a lady friend to do such things—the needlework is quite awful."

Marty's expression changed to a sneer. "You!" he exclaimed. "I thought I'd—"

"Sent me to a hospital?" Keel laughed. "You did, Marty; they sent me home. You left hardly a bruise. Hardly a bruise."

The comment, aimed to stir Marty's wrath, had the desired effect. Snorting, the three thugs began to move forward. This time, however, Keel was ready for them. His clenched fist smashed into Alfie's stomach. The thick man wheezed as his breath spat out, and he staggered back. Marty's hand went toward his pocket, but Keel spun around, kicking the thug hard on the shins.

This allowed the third man time to move. Keel managed to duck low and avoid the blow, then grabbed the arm and heaved. The off-balance man went sprawling. By now, Alfie had regained his breath. Spinning on his heel, Keel gave him a sharp, hard-handed jab in the solar plexus. All the color drained from Alfie's face and he sank heavily to the ground with a grunt. Marty made another motion toward his pocket, but Keel saw it from the corner of his eye. Whipping about, he landed a punch to Marty's chin that sent a juddering shock up his arm. Marty reeled back, cracking his head on a low wall near a little shrubbery, and crashed to the ground.

The man on the ground was trying to get up, bleeding in several spots from where the sharp gravel had gashed him. Without mercy, Keel slammed his heel down on the man's hand. The thug screamed, and Keel heard something snap.

Seeing Marty attempt to get up, Keel grabbed a handful of the man's shirt and jerked him roughly to his feet. Though he was panting from exertion, not one of the men had laid a hand on him. "Right," he gasped, "now let's have some information, Marty."

"Put me mate down," said a youngish voice from the pub doorway. Keel glanced back and saw that the six young thugs were filing out. All were ominously quiet, save for the one who had issued the order. "You 'eard me," the youth repeated. "Put 'im down." Behind him, one of his mates was slipping on a knuckle duster; another was unwinding a length of bicycle chain. The spokesman was ostentatiously cleaning his nails with a flick knife. So they were with Marty, after all.

The youngster flipped the knife into his palm and tested the sharpness of the blade with the ball of his thumb. Keel did as he was told, pushing Marty from him and back into the shrubbery. The six youths began to close in, and Keel knew he was in very serious trouble now. Three unarmed, boozed-up men were one thing—but six punks, all armed with various nasty items, was quite a different matter.

"That's quite far enough," said another voice. This time it came from a woman, who stood resolutely behind the thugs. She had appeared from one of the back doors without anyone having seen her. She was dressed in olive-green leather, and her expression was anything but ladylike. She looked contemptuously from one young thug to the next. "Time to stop playing with the big boys. Go home and get your noses wiped," she sneered.

The leader of the gang made a quick decision. Unhappy about fighting two opponents, he gestured for two of his men to take on the woman. He and the rest moved back toward Keel.

That was a very serious mistake.

Cathy Gale had absolutely no intention of waiting for the punks to reach her. One of them, a ginger-haired brat with a broken nose, started toward her, swinging a bicycle chain. The other had a knife. Cathy realized the chain had the longer reach and could do her serious damage if its wielder used it, so she went for him first. She simply ran a few paces, then jumped, feet first. The startled youth barely had time to scream before her feet smacked into his chest and he went down. He didn't get up. Rolling forward, Cathy somersaulted to her feet, using the downed thug as a springboard.

The kid with the knife was stunned—he had never seen a woman fight like this. He obviously thought that all women ever did was scream and pull hair. Not this one. This silent bitch moved toward him. Was she mad? Grinning, he hefted the knife he carried and lunged at her. Normally this would have awed anyone, but this crazy female just sighed, low and contemptuously. She reached out a hand, plucking the lid from the nearest dustbin. Thinking she was going to use it as a shield, he dived forward—and the hurtling lid smacked into his face. He staggered for a moment, then continued his forward momentum, hitting the wall with a crunch. His jaw had been shattered by the projectile and he was out cold.

The events had happened so swiftly that the other four thugs hadn't even reached Keel when they realized that something had gone very badly wrong. One glanced over his shoulder. He saw Cathy running toward them and the other two members of the gang out for the count. He yelled a warning to his mates.

Cathy launched herself through the air, catching two of the gang high on their chests, using them to cushion her fall. By now, the astounded Keel had galvanized himself into motion and jumped the gang leader. He grabbed the kid's arm and twisted it, and the knife clattered to the ground from the kid's senseless fingers. Still holding the arm, Keel slammed the youth into the nearest wall, then released his hold. The punk slid down the wall, leaving a bloody smear on the bricks.

The last gang member took in the scene with a shocked, pale-faced stare. Looking at Cathy, he shrieked, then turned and ran for his life.

Keel watched with some amusement as Cathy made short chopping motions at the necks of the two fallen thugs. She straightened up. With a slight smile of satisfaction, she brushed back her hair and then held out a hand to Keel.

Still amazed by what he had witnessed, Keel shook the hand warmly. "David Keel," he offered, surveying the five gang members and the three crooks he had earlier settled with.

"Cathy Gale," she told him. "Did you find out what you wanted yet from Marty?"

Keel had entirely forgotten his original intention. He could hold off questioning her as to how she knew about him until later. "Not yet—but I suspect he'll be more forthcoming now," he grunted, and headed for his victim.

Marty was dazed, but conscious enough to have witnessed most of the short fight. He held up his hands as if to fend them off. "Okay," he managed to gasp as Keel hauled him to his feet. "No more, please."

Keel grinned, but there was no humor in the smile. "Right," he said. "Where's Dr. Crowles?"

"I took him to a factory," Marty told him between pauses for breath. "We were paid to do it. Nothing personal."

"Knight Industries in Crawley?"

Marty nodded, not even surprised that Keel knew. "Yeah."

"Who paid you?" asked Cathy.

"Dunno, miss. I never met him. He rang the office." Marty jerked his thumb toward the pub. "He gave me Cowles's address, told me to put the snatch on him. We had to deliver him to the factory gate, and we'd be met and paid. We did the job, and we were met by this big, ugly brute. He was over seven feet tall . . ."

Keel had heard enough, and wasn't up to hearing any lying claims from Marty. Turning on his heels, Keel started back for his car. "I hope they were all paid," he grunted as Cathy fell in beside him. "They'll need it to repair their car."

"And to buy bandages." Cathy smiled. "Meanwhile, how do you feel about an exchange of information? I'm going after Knight Industries myself."

Pausing outside his car door, Keel examined the woman. Pretty—very pretty—but tough, too. And she clearly had some stake in this affair; she hadn't helped him against that gang simply because she liked his looks. But why should she want to help him? He threw open the passenger door. "Get in," he suggested. "We can talk on the way there."

"I have my own car, but I'm sure it'll be safe, parked here." She nodded her head back at the fallen fighters. "I think the message will get around." She climbed in beside him as he started the car. "I believe we have a mutual friend. John Steed."

For the first time since she'd met him, Keel gave a genuine hearty laugh, and then shook his head in disbelief. "I should have known you'd be one of Steed's friends. He always did like dangerous women. *Beautiful* and dangerous women."

"Thank you, David," she answered, taking the comment as a compliment. "Now I think it's time we compared notes . . ."

10 Messing About on the River

Steed steered the Bentley with ease down the long, winding roads. He and Emma had left the confines of London behind and were heading farther up the Thames to the point where the Soviet agents had pinpointed Mother. Emma, sitting in the passenger seat, stole a look at Steed. His familiar face was alight with the thrill of the hunt. It brought back memories of many similar days in the past. Briefly, she wondered why it had seemed so important to her to give up those days.

She was filled with an excitement that she hadn't felt in a year, somewhat akin to the emotions that Steed was obviously experiencing—but stronger, she suspected. Well, Steed hadn't taken a break from his work in years. Come to think of it, he *lived* for the game; she felt sure that he had never given any thought to retirement. Perhaps after this one . . . ? But no—the look on Steed's face said it all: he was alert to the thrill of danger. True, she thought, there was a thrill in the business world, the delicate negotiating of contracts, the development of new designs, the encouraging of productivity. Emma enjoyed her role in all of that, and she was definitely good at her job. Now, though, in the crisp air of the English countryside, on the trail of some unknown foe, trees whipping past almost in a blur . . . it was like being drunk, in a way. It felt surreal, more than the everyday grind of life. Suddenly she was aware of how much she'd missed this life, having picked up the gauntlet their enemy had flung down and taken her place beside Steed again.

Could she bear to go back to the factories after this? While Peter was alive, she had felt a need for more security, for a calmer job—the exact opposite of Peter's own career. He had lived to fly, and the farther, the faster, the higher, the better. Even being lost in South America for two years had, if anything, intensified his love of flying. He had crawled away from one shattered plane, and as soon as he was declared fit again, he went back into the cockpit of the first bird he could harness.

He hadn't walked away from that next crash.

It had been bitter enough when she had thought him dead the first time; the second time proved unbearable. She had needed support then, and had hoped that Steed would come. He never did, of course, and she had believed she could never forgive him for that. Now here she was, beside him again, as though nothing had changed.

To her shock, she found that nothing *had*

changed. When she first accepted his offer to become his partner, her husband was thought dead, and she had been bored with an endless stream of parties—bored and lacking in direction. Steed had come along, infuriating and charming her but offering her work that he was convinced no one else could do. Their times together had been full of danger and giddy excitement, never boredom or lack of direction. Always that challenge: "Mrs. Peel, we're needed." Then it was off into the fray, like latter-day knights errant.

Now Peter was dead—and she knew that this was exactly what she had been waiting for, perhaps even secretly praying for: Steed to arrive, and with his winning smile, lead her off to . . . what? What new threat or danger would lie at the end of this journey?

But this time was different; it couldn't last. She wasn't really here as Steed's partner, but as a temporary replacement for Tara King. For good reasons, Steed couldn't use Tara this time—but the next? Emma knew that it would be Tara to whom he turned. This one adventure, this glorious time, this was it. After this was over, she'd be back in the factories, organizing the wavefront of British industry. She hoped she could survive that without a broken spirit. Her only option was to savor every second of this adventure, and to be ready to walk back into the shadows.

She jerked back to reality with a jolt. How could she harbor resentment against Tara? It was wrong to dislike the other woman for having what she wanted. She had met Tara only the once, on the day that she had parted from Steed. A nice girl, she'd thought, if slightly overweight. Well, a few months of dashing about with Steed must have changed that! Emma had made her choices, and had to stick with them.

Didn't she?

Steed, oblivious to her thoughts, laughed out loud. "Just like the old days, Mrs. Peel," he exclaimed. "The open roads, the roaring Bentley, the quest ahead."

"You forgot the champagne," Emma joked, trying to bury her thoughts.

"It's in the back," Steed told her, taking her comment at face value. "When I was a Boy Scout, they told me to always be prepared. I learned my lesson well."

"I don't think they had champagne in mind, Steed."

"Well, more fools they, then!" He grinned. "When this is all over, we'll have to crack the bottle for old times' sake."

"After we've told Mother about what's going on?" asked Emma. "Then what? Do you have any leads on who's behind it?"

"Not one," Steed told her cheerfully. "But I'm sure we'll come up with something. We always do."

"Always the optimist," remarked Emma.

Steed grinned at her in reply. He took the next corner almost on two wheels, and ahead of them was the gleam of sunlight on the river. Willows hung heavily over the water, trailing their leaves into the dark, sluggish stream. Sunlight filtered through the trees, giving the river a greenish cast.

"Perfect spot for a picnic," Steed commented. "Perhaps we'll invite Mother . . ."

"You're prepared for that, too?"

He beamed. "Hamper in the trunk. Freshly stocked, and just waiting for two healthy appetites."

"*That* part I'm prepared for," Emma replied.

Spotting a small lane leading into the field by the river, Steed drew the Bentley up there and came to a halt facing the water. Leaving the engine running, he stood up in his seat, gripping the top of the windshield. Emma noticed that he seemed a trifle agitated. "No sign of the submarine," he murmured.

"I'm not surprised," Emma said. "It isn't like Mother to be conspicuous."

"No," agreed Steed. "It isn't." He didn't elaborate on this. Instead, he vaulted over the door and onto the grass. He picked up his umbrella from the backseat, straightened his bowler, and flashed her a smile. "I'll just take a quick look."

Emma was convinced that there was something troubling him. Instead of staying still, she too vaulted out of the car and fell in behind him. He didn't look back or say a word.

It was a short walk to the river, and Steed stopped at the edge, looking upstream, then down. There was nothing in sight, not even a rowboat, which, thought Steed, was highly unusual for a delightful stretch of water on such a beautiful day.

"Maybe Brodny's information was wrong?" Emma suggested, coming to a halt beside Steed.

"I'd be very surprised if it was," Steed told her cryptically. He continued to scan the water and then pointed.

About thirty feet downstream, a rippling had begun in the bottle-green river. As they watched, a periscope broke surface, followed by a small conning tower, and finally the lines of a sleek submarine. It was some thirty feet long and rather fat. The conning tower was low, standing no more than six feet from the deck, and there were no markings at all on the craft. It began to move toward them slowly, and then the hatch in the tower popped open.

A blond head appeared, followed by a good part of Rhonda's body. She filled the top of the tower and waved to them both to come aboard.

"Trouble," Steed muttered.

Emma was puzzled. "What do you mean?"

"Take a look at that submarine. If Rhonda just fits, then how could Mother get aboard?"

Her adrenaline pumping, Emma realized that Steed was correct; someone of Mother's impressive bulk could never have gotten inside the submarine—and yet there was Rhonda, without whom he never went anywhere.

"You knew that this was a trap," she hissed.

"Guessed," he corrected. "We needed a lead on the villains behind this whole thing. I was suspicious when I saw this location. Mother hates to be more than twenty minutes from Westminster; the Minister complains too much if he is late for an appointment."

The submarine was drawing closer as they talked. Emma was ready to go aboard, but Steed made no move. "Are we just going to stand here?" she asked.

"I want it closer to the shore," he told her. "When I tell you, sprint back to the Bentley."

"Whatever you say," Emma agreed. Experience

had taught her never to challenge Steed's judgment in such situations.

Rhonda—or whoever it was—jumped stiffly down from the conning tower to the deck, as if making ready to moor or to welcome them both aboard. As always, she was perfectly silent and perfectly impassive. When the craft was almost touching the riverbank, Steed yelled: "Go!"

Emma turned and sprinted for the Bentley. Much faster than Steed, she arrived there first and ground to a halt with her hand resting on the radiator cap. She wiped her hair out of her eyes and peered back. Steed was running toward her in a zigzag fashion as fast as he could, and Rhonda was close behind him, her long legs eating up the ground. She was obviously not chasing Steed to say hello. Behind them on the river, a small hatch in the submarine's nose was opening up.

Surveying Steed's plight with some bemusement, Emma headed back directly for Rhonda. She passed Steed, who made it to the Bentley safely, and then threw herself at his pursuer.

Swinging her foot into Rhonda's shinbone, Emma threw herself backward onto the ground, drawing her right leg upward around the blonde's left ankle. With her left leg, she kicked Rhonda's kneecap with all of the strength she could muster. The double-foot-lever throw, absolutely guaranteed to shatter an opponent's kneecap.

Rhonda remained erect, apparently unaffected.

Emma slid through Rhonda's arms as the blonde bent down to throttle her, and dropped into a wary crouch, her eyes firmly fixed on those of her opponent.

Rhonda moved, very swiftly. Emma pirouetted and kicked out. To her shock, Rhonda caught her ankle and flipped her into the air. For a brief second, Emma was totally disoriented, but then she hit the ground and rolled with the blow. Nevertheless, she was winded, and Rhonda moved back in again for the kill.

The shock had not been that Rhonda was so fast or so proficient, but that the fingers that had gripped Emma were not human. They were more like metal claws, and the agonizing pain in Emma's ankle bore witness to the fact that she was not fighting a human opponent. This "Rhonda" was a fake, a robot of some kind. Some very lethal kind.

Steed, meanwhile, had kept his attention on the submarine. There was no need to worry about Mrs. Peel; she could always handle herself. From the open hatch came a small deck gun, unmanned but not unloaded. It moved by remote control to target Steed, and opened fire. Steed dived behind his beloved Bentley and heard bullets slamming into the doors and hood. He winced. "Another paint job," he muttered to himself. Crouching low, he sidled around to the vehicle's trunk and opened it. Keeping himself covered as best he could, he groped around the back and into the dark interior. His fingers closed on what he was searching for, and he dragged it out.

The small rocket launcher had been "borrowed" from an Army ordnance factory Steed had visited on his way to see Mrs. Peel. It was an experimental shoulder-held device that looked very much like a bazooka. Instead of launching a shell, though, this device fired a rocket. Bullets still slammed about him as Steed popped up behind the protection of the car, aimed and fired.

The recoil threw him from his feet. Falling backward, he drew his arms about his head in a weak attempt to stave off the bullets that whined past his ears.

A terrific blast and a sheet of flame followed. The ground shook. Steed peered out through the spoked wheels of the Bentley and saw the remnants of the miniature submarine, blazing away. A direct hit! The deck gun had fallen silent, hanging crookedly from its supports now, and the conning tower was a small inferno. Steed was certain that there was no chance of any survivors.

The unexpected blast as Steed's rocket destroyed the submarine had caught "Rhonda" off guard. Emma, on her back on the ground, had been better protected. Bits of flying metal sprayed about them. Emma was unhit, but one chunk smacked into the robot Rhonda's face. It carried away skin and hair, leaving exposed metal.

Emma used the moment to her own advantage. She managed to regain her feet and, picking up a hefty fallen branch, jabbed at the robot. It hardly faltered. A short, sharp chop from the hand shattered the end of the branch. Emma halted her advance. A similar blow to her person would shatter bones and quite possibly kill her. Using the wood to keep the robot at bay, Emma started to circle it.

"Rhonda" was not content to wait. It began to push forward, forcing Emma to retreat as she considered her next move. She was being forced backward, closer to the river and into the tangle of trees there. Perhaps . . . The robot lashed out, sending the broken branch spinning from Emma's hands. Then it jumped forward, reaching for her throat.

Emma jumped vertically. Her hands grabbed a branch and she swung her feet up. The robot passed just below her, surprised by the move. It halted, corrected, then turned to try again. Emma, her gymnastic training coming into play, switched her hands, spinning about to face the robot. As it reached out for her, Emma swung her body in a tight arc. Her feet connected with the half-metal head. The robot rocked under the blow, and Emma's feet swung backward. As she swung forward again, Emma released her hold on the branch.

She hit the robot like a missile herself, knocking it off balance and down. Landing lightly on her feet, Emma grabbed for the fallen branch again and slammed it down like a spear, through the "head" of the creature. It entered the broken gap there and continued through. Components smashed, and a stench of burning hit Emma's nostrils. Sparks danced across the robot's face. Emma twisted the stick and heard further damage.

The robot twitched, trying to get to its feet, but it was badly damaged. Grabbing a rock, Emma pounded down on the "head," feeling a great deal of satisfaction at the ringing of metal as it collapsed under her blows. Finally, the robot was still. Dropping the stone—by now dripping with oil—Emma stood up and brushed the hair from her eyes.

"Well done, Mrs. Peel!" Steed called, crossing to join her. He no longer held the missile launcher, but Emma could see it where it lay on the grass. In the river, hissing and steaming, the small submarine was breaking apart and sinking.

"Was that a part of your Boy Scout training, too?" she asked as her breathing returned to normal.

"Of course!" he told her. "I earned two merit badges in rocketry, you know." Suddenly serious, he told her: "When I heard from Brodny about the submarine, I decided to come prepared."

"So you picked that up at Selfridges?" she asked.

"Exactly! Even got a discount." He stared down at the broken robot. "It's familiar, wouldn't you say?"

"Very," Emma admitted, chilled. "It looks like a Cybernaut. But it can't be."

On his knee, Steed poked at the exposed circuits with the ferrule of his umbrella. "A new generation of Cybernauts," he agreed. "Ones that look like people we know—and act like them. These are sophisticated, Mrs. Peel. Very sophisticated."

Emma thought back to their previous two encounters with the Cybernauts. They had been cold, emotionless robots, built by the crippled Dr. Armstrong. Powerful, silent, and programmable, they had twice been turned against her and Steed. The first time had been by Armstrong, and the second time by the late inventor's brother, Paul Beresford. But Armstrong had died, killed accidentally by one of his own creations.

"How can they be?" she objected. "Armstrong was killed." She didn't like where Steed's thoughts seemed to be heading.

"So were the Cybernauts," Steed said softly. "But machines can't die."

"Armstrong was a man," Emma insisted.

"I wonder . . ." Steed was lost in thought. Then his umbrella flicked out at the ground. "What do we have here?" He stood up, a small item impaled on his umbrella point. He transferred the object to his palm and stared at it thoughtfully. After a moment's silence, he passed it over to Emma.

She took the object from Steed. A chill passed through her. It was a small transistorized circuit, one that she knew well. Though burned at one corner, the name on the circuit was quite legible: KNIGHT INDUSTRIES.

"It looks as though I am involved more deeply than I thought," Emma remarked casually.

Steed grinned cheerfully. "How much would you like to bet that it's from your factory at Crawley?"

"I never bet on a certainty," Emma replied. "Especially given that Dr. Armstrong's first great aim in life was to automate factory assembly lines."

"He's buried in Highgate Cemetery," said Steed.

"Our next stop?" The game was well and truly afoot by now.

"Yes, and then on to Crawley," Steed confirmed, straightening his bowler.

As they climbed into the Bentley, Steed's eyes fell on the lines of bullet holes that had peppered the car's sides. "She'll never forgive me." He sighed. Seeing Emma's blank stare, he patted the dash. "Poor old thing. I believe the time has come when it would be better to leave her at home with the Rolls. The opposition cares nothing for her noble vintage lines."

Emma fought back a smile; Steed and his cars! He lavished the praise upon them that other men would reserve for wives and family.

Steed released the clutch and took off the hand brake. Backing out onto the road, he said: "I'd feel a lot happier if I knew for certain that Armstrong is resting quietly in his grave."

A chill passed through Emma at the thought. "And if he isn't?"

"Boy Scouts to the rescue again." Steed laughed, seemingly unaffected. "I've also got a whole string of garlic cloves in the back."

Emma could almost believe it.

11 You Never Know Who You Can Trust These Days

Tara's sense of hearing had almost returned to normal by the time she drew her car to a halt outside Steed's Stable Mews apartment. There was no sign of the Bentley or the Rolls, but if he was home, they would most likely be parked around the back. She took the stairs two at a time, then turned right and stopped outside the olive-green front door. It bore no number, just a push bell positioned in the right doorjamb, above which sat a card bearing the legend JOHN STEED. Mentally crossing her fingers, Tara rang the bell.

After a moment, the door opened and Steed smiled out at her. "Tara! What a pleasant surprise. Do come in." He opened the door wider and she ambled in past him. Since he wasn't wearing his jacket and tie, she presumed he was in the process of dressing to go out.

Crossing the pine-paneled room, she elected to sit on the red leather-upholstered settee. Where should she begin? The words tumbled out of her mouth, staccato style. "Steed, I've been ordered to kill you."

"Have I been a naughty boy?" His face registered no change at the news.

"Someone wants us to think that you have. A telephone call to Mother from an agent named Harrison was cut off when he was killed—supposedly by you."

"Do you believe it, Tara?"

"Of course not, Steed—and neither does Mother. That's why he gave me the case—I must be the only agent he can trust not to obey orders and kill you on sight."

Steed smiled again. "Well, that's a relief. Would you? Kill me, I mean?"

"If there were undeniable proof of your guilt, and no other way—yes."

"And the phone call? I presume Mother had it taped? Wasn't that sufficient proof?"

"It looked that way, but I had it processed by a Professor Lipp at V.O.I.C.E., and he managed to prove that your voice had been cleverly faked on the phone."

"A setup," Steed commented thoughtfully. "But by whom? Do you have any leads?"

"Yes. Lipp recognized the voice synthesizer used to mimic your voice on the phone as one he made, with help and funds from a man employed by Knight Industries."

"You have been busy," said Steed softly. "Do we know the man's name?"

"Well, no." Tara explained succinctly what had happened at the house.

"I see." Steed looked thoughtful. "So Lipp is dead?"

"No, he'll recover presently—homeless but unabashed. He's gritty enough to start over." Seeing the frown on Steed's face, Tara hurried him along. "Hadn't we better drive out to Knight Industries and try to clear your name? It's a really good copy of your voice, Steed, and anyone who can make that can cause even more trouble whenever he likes." She took the tape out of her handbag and passed it over to him. "Listen for yourself."

Steed took the tape and then looked around, momentarily uncertain. Suddenly Tara became very, very worried. This person didn't know where Steed kept his tape deck . . .

Rising to her feet, she crossed to the window and stood by the drapes. Inches from her hands was a bronze mandarin figure that Steed kept on the windowsill.

"It's not just the voice, is it?" she asked quietly, taking hold of the statuette. "It's *Steed* that he's copied—"

The man made a swift lunge at her, but Tara lashed out with the mandarin, catching him full in the face. The bronze clattered to the floor, but the attacker barely paused. Her handbag came next. She brought it swinging up into the man's jaw. The leather stitching split, showering her assailant with the contents. Her compact burst open, releasing a film of pink face powder into the man's face. The false Steed's legs caught on the coffee table and he fell. Tara lashed down at his neck, finishing his fall to the floor. Momentarily blinded, he rolled onto his back and, with a startling burst of speed, kicked out at her ankles. She tried to move, but the man's feet became entangled in her own. In a blaze of pain, she collapsed backward onto Steed's armchair. It felt like she'd been kicked by a mule.

The imposter jerked to his feet and lunged at her. Tara twisted and dived over the arm of the seat. She hit the floor and found herself backed up against the table that stood in the window alcove. Next to her stood the tuba with the fresh flowers. She snatched the flowers out and tossed them into her assailant's face as he jumped for her again. He batted them aside and kept on coming. The move had bought Tara an extra second or two, and she was ready for him. As he lunged again, she brought up the empty tuba, ramming it solidly down over his head.

The force of his impact slammed her back against the wall, but he was unable to control his forward momentum. With a shattering of glass and wood, he fell straight through the window. There was a crunch from outside, and then silence.

Breathing heavily, Tara staggered to the broken window, kicking aside shards of glass as she did so. The tuba still rammed over his head, the mysterious intruder lay very still in the street. His legs straddled the metal horse posts that sat on either side of the front entrance. It had been a fall of some twenty feet, and he was either unconscious or dead. Perhaps now she would get some answers.

She ran down the stairs, still amazed by the intruder's resemblance to the real Steed. She had been completely taken in by him—the right mannerisms, the right inflections in his voice, everything but the knowledge that Steed possessed. No wonder the person behind this had managed to frame Steed and fool the Department so easily. The inventor was a genius—demented, perhaps, but clever enough to escape detection until now. She had to discover how it had been done—and if there were more duplicates like this one on the loose.

The body still lay where it had fallen, fragments of glass and wood scattered about. Thankfully, this was a very quiet section of town, and there were as yet no onlookers. Tara wondered what the real Steed would have to say about the destruction of his flat. Her eyes caught sight of a smashed brass stable lamp that swung precariously from the end of its electric cable above the entrance. It had been a gift from Mrs. Gale; its destruction would not make him happy. Tara walked over to where the fake Steed lay and started to bend down to check his pulse.

Without warning, the man jerked upward, threw the tuba off his head and grabbed for her arm. Off balance, Tara found her arm clutched in a viselike grip, and then the other hand came for her face. She ducked, and the arm narrowly missed her. Knowing this was no time to be delicate or ladylike, she kicked the imposter right between the legs.

He didn't even blink, but Tara felt as if she had broken her foot. He must be wearing armor under his clothes! The pressure on her arm increased and she was forced to her knees in pain. Her attacker seemed to be enjoying her humiliation and agony. The pressure on her wrist increased, and she knew something would break soon—and it wouldn't be his grip. Fighting back both a scream and tears, she glanced at the ground and saw a large spearhead of glass from the window. Snatching it up with her free hand, she slashed up at his face.

The glass scored a deep furrow up his cheek before it embedded itself firmly in his eye. She expected a flood of blood and ichor, but it never came. Instead, the attacker released her, pawing at his face. The pressure off her hand, she pulled back, fast.

She stared at the rut she had scored across the man's cheek. The skin where she had slashed it hung in shreds, exposing bare metal underneath. The glass sliver was lodged in an eye that was obviously electronic. She had penetrated it, cutting several wires, which hung loosely. Sparks flashed in the exposed gap. The "man" was a robot!

The robot tore the glass shard from its eye and started for her. Tara turned and ran, barely thinking. How could she beat this unstoppable creature? Feet pounding, she simply ran as fast as she could. She could hear the robot behind her; it sounded like it was catching up.

Out of the corner of her eye she saw a small park, and twisted to dive in through the iron gates. She turned in mid-stride and saw the robot barely ten feet behind her. Wrenching the wrought-iron gate from its rest, she slammed it in the creature's direction, hard.

It caught the mechanism in full stride, dropping it to the ground. The gate swung back toward her, and she held her breath. Shaking slightly, the robot clambered to its feet. Gripping the gate, it lifted the metal high above its head and then flung it aside onto the grass. Its clothing was shredded, and more of the plastic skin that covered it was torn. One arm gleamed metallically in the light, and another portion of the face was destroyed, taking with it the uncanny resemblance to Steed. Something had come loose from the shoulder of the robot, and she could see the exposed circuitry there. But it was still able to function, and it started after her again.

She ran once more, her fear helping her to keep going. The robot continued the relentless pursuit, pounding its way along the gravel path. She ran without a plan, knowing that she would tire before the robot would stop, and desperately hoping for inspiration.

Breaking through a small fringe of trees, she barely came to a halt, her arms windmilling, before she ran right into a duck pond. As she wavered, the robot hurtled out of the trees and slammed its full weight into her. Iron fingers clawed for her throat as they both went face-first into the pond.

It wasn't deep, but that hardly mattered. The heavy robot was on top of her, its fingers clenching about her throat. In a haze of red, Tara realized that it was trying to drown her. Fighting to stop the air in her lungs from exploding up her throat, Tara scrabbled about in the mud and muck at the bottom of the pond. Her fingers closed about something hard—a rock! Dragging her hand up through the water, she slammed up as hard as she could with it. She felt it hit somewhere, and then the robot bore down harder. The water was filthy, and she could see nothing at all. There was simply a terrible weight on her, the merciless hands about her neck, and the incredible, burning pain in her lungs.

Frantically, she twisted. The robot was unbalanced, and she managed to get her head above water for a second or two. Gasping, she took a mouthful of air and filthy water as the robot strove to push her back. She could see the exposed circuits in its shoulder now, and an idea finally sprang to her mind. As the creature forced her head backward again, she brought up her left hand, clenching a fistful of oozing slime, and hit the shoulder with it, rubbing hard into the electronic circuitry.

All movement stopped for a second, then a series of short jerks rocked the thing. Her head went under again, but she managed to regain the surface. A series of sparks arced across the exposed wiring as the sludge shorted out everything it touched. Tara prised the hands from about her neck and staggered to her feet. The water was barely up to her knees.

The robot sparked and fizzed, blue lights dancing inside it. Then, in a small shower of flames, it collapsed forward into the water and lay still.

Tara wiped her filthy hair, then her face, and stood there, taking deep, thankful breaths until she was steady and able to move again. She started back the few feet to the shore, then became aware of another figure. She fell into a fighting crouch before she realized it was one of the park groundsmen.

" 'Ere!" he exclaimed, his walruslike mustache bristling savagely. "Can't you read? There's no paddlin' allowed in 'ere, me lass!"

Tara dragged herself back onto dry land, feeling

an absolute mess. "Don't tell me," she muttered. "Tell him." She pointed at where the robot was fizzling away in the water.

"And there's no litterin', either!" the keeper snarled. "Fetch it out."

Tara looked up at him and sighed.

This definitely wasn't one of her better days.

12 Trespassers Will Be Electrocuted

"It's somewhat odd," Cathy Gale commented as Keel drove on in silence. A sign notifying them that they were ten miles from Crawley flashed past the car. Keel switched on the lights as darkness marched relentlessly down.

He glanced at his watch. Almost seven. It seemed as though the events of the day should have eaten away more hours than that. "What is?" he finally asked in response to Cathy's remark.

"That you and I should both have worked at one time with Steed. That we both should be heading for Katawa. That we should both get sidetracked into this business with Knight Industries. If I believed in coincidence, I'd say that the gods of fate must be working overtime."

Keel kept his eyes on the road, but risked a quick

glimpse into the rearview mirror. He could see Cathy's face perfectly, and she definitely looked tense. "Then let's pray that they're on our side."

"There's an old saying I like," she said by way of a reply. "Once is happenstance; twice is coincidence. Three times is enemy action."

Keel considered his own response carefully. "I tried calling Steed myself. There was no reply."

Cathy flashed a brief, strained smile. "I tried the same thing, with the same result. He'll be mixed up in this, though. I'd bet on it."

"No takers. Unless Steed has changed, we're bound to bump into him somewhere down the line." Keel grinned. "In Steed's business, anything that seems coincidental is definitely enemy action. Still, I can't see a link between the kidnapping of Cowles and the murderous attacks of a robot gorilla."

"And the fact that you and I are linked to Katawa *and* to Steed?" asked Cathy.

"Mmmm. That does make me suspicious."

"Then I'll provide you with another piece of the jigsaw puzzle," Cathy offered. "Knight Industries used to be owned by a Knight; the owner now is one Mrs. Emma Peel."

"So?"

"Would you like to guess who replaced me as Steed's assistant?"

Keel's eyes narrowed as he considered this additional information. Coincidences be damned—this *was* planned. "You're saying that Cowles's kidnapping was planned?" he said, thinking it out as he spoke.

"Something like that, yes," Cathy replied.

"And the card that I snatched from Marty was a plant. Left behind to lead me to—"

"—get you to the Crawley plant," Cathy agreed.

"But the gorilla! How could anyone know that you'd become involved in that? Or find that piece of fur with Knight's name on it?"

"I don't know," Cathy said. "Perhaps that side of things was a coincidence? It would take a phenomenal mind to *plan* everything that has happened." Then she laughed. "I seem to recall that phenomenal minds and Steed go hand in hand."

"Yes. That's what worries me," Keel confessed. He suddenly slammed on the brakes and pulled to the side of the road. Cathy's first thought was that there was trouble, but everything seemed normal. "Telephone box," said Keel, pointing just ahead of them. "I just want to check up on a hunch of mine. Hang on."

Watching him move away into the circle of light cast by the booth, Cathy had to admire him. She could see the pent-up energy in his body, the way he held himself ready for anything. It was easy to see why Steed had enjoyed working with this man. He held a promise of danger and challenge—and yet, at the same time, a hint of compassion and humanity. An interesting man, all told. And very handsome. Who knew, when this was all over . . .

Keel grinned without any real humor when he returned from making his call. "I just spoke to someone at Knight's main office in London, a Dr. Carruthers. Seems that Mrs. Peel left earlier. If you need more than one guess as to who she'd just met . . ."

"So this is all something to do with Steed," Cathy breathed. "Which means . . ."

"That we'd be wise to proceed with caution when we reach Crawley," Keel finished for her. He started up the car again. "This is obviously a trap."

"Yes." Cathy turned to face him. "But are we the prey—or just the bait?"

"Good question." He didn't try to answer it, concentrating on his driving instead. He had looked at a map of the area earlier and knew where he was heading. On the outskirts of the town, he turned off into a large industrial estate. The headlights flashed over a sign bearing Knight's name before he shut them and the engine off. "All ashore that's going ashore," he said softly.

As Cathy climbed out of the car, Keel reached into the glove compartment. He took out a heavy-duty flashlight, a roll of thick tape, and a gun. The latter he slipped into his pocket without a word. Tearing strips from the tape, he masked most of the flashlight's glass. When he tested it, it gave off a faint glow—just enough for them to see by, but not enough to alert any guards. Then he locked the car and joined her.

The night was getting cool now, but Cathy's leather fighting gear was very warm, and the adrenaline in her bloodstream prevented any hint of the cold from reaching her. She was back in the firing line again, steeling herself for any emergency. Keel appeared to be equally calm, but she knew he had to be feeling the charge of danger in his own blood. Neither of them had been involved in an adventure like this since they had broken with Steed, but those were never forgotten. "Stay alert at all times—and never, *never* take anything at face value, Mrs. Gale." Steed's words echoed in her brain once again. Silently, she and Keel padded across the road and toward the factory.

It lay on a large area of cleared ground. Most of the other units in this industrial park were surrounded by large lawns and small fences. The Knight complex sat on bare concrete, and a ten-foot wire-mesh fence encompassed the perimeter. As they approached this, their eyes picked out two strands of thin wire strung along the top. The fence was supported by metal ribs, each carefully topped with ceramic insulators. They approached it with caution.

"Trespassers will be electrocuted," Cathy murmured.

In the near darkness, she could see the barest hint of amusement in Keel's eyes. "But we aren't trespassers," he replied. He took a small white plastic card from his wallet. She saw the Knight logo on it, and a thin black strip. "Magnetic key," he explained.

Edging along the fence, they approached the main gate warily, but there was no sign of a guard. The whole blocklike building was bathed in darkness that left it stark against the black sky. There were no windows at all, and only a single main doorway opposite the gate. The gate had no need of a guard. Instead of a lock, it had a small box attached to its middle. It had a slit in it, and a small light, currently lit in a burning red. After scanning the area a moment, Keel inserted the plastic card into the slot. There was a low hum, then the light blinked green. They heard the sound of a bolt being withdrawn. Cathy and Keel exchanged glances and he pushed at the gate.

It swung slowly and silently open. Retrieving the entry card, Keel led the way through the gate. It closed behind them with a click of an electric motor.

The time it took to cross twenty feet from the gate to the doorway seemed almost endless. Keel felt naked in the open, as though eyes were watching their progress. He was correct in this feeling. What he and Cathy couldn't see was that a security camera was trained on them from the top of the fence. It had been following their actions for quite a while now, its miniature lens completely unaffected by the darkness.

Inside the building, a man sat watching Keel and Cathy on the television monitor as they approached the main door. The unseen observer laughed quietly to himself. "So they both came together?" he mused aloud. "A bonus. Two birds with one bullet. That makes things simpler. I do hope they aren't too bothered by the lack of a reception committee."

"How far do you intend to let them get?" asked a second presence. This voice had a curious, flat, metallic sound to it. It sounded only half human. The other half . . .

The observer spun about in his chair, smiling. "Oh, far enough for them to find out a little of what is going on," he said cheerfully. "It'll make it so much more interesting when we kill them."

The exterior door had opened as easily as the main gate had. They slid inside and closed the door softly. Their eyes slowly adjusted to the lack of light. The interior of the factory was completely dark, which was understandable at this time of the night. Keel eased his flashlight up, then turned it on. A soft, brownish light emerged from its taped-up lens, helping them to see a little.

They were standing in the foyer of the factory. A door to their left had a time clock next to it and obviously led to the main work area. A second door was next to a frosted-glass window. The reception desk. The third door was marked PRIVATE. Cathy gave a crooked smile and tried the knob. It was locked. Fishing in a zipped pocket, she brought out a set of skeleton keys. Keel held the light close to the offending lock while admiring her readiness. When Steed trains them, he thought, they stay trained. She estimated the key she'd need. The first one didn't do the trick, but the second worked perfectly. She straightened up, but Keel brushed past her, entering the room first.

He swept the muted light about it. A desk, two glass-fronted bookshelves, and a filing cabinet were the main items in the room. There was a small table lamp on the desk, and no windows. Keel gestured for Cathy to shut the door, and then he turned on the lamp.

The sudden flood of light hurt their eyes. They blinked rapidly until they were used to the new level of illumination. Keel then started to check out the desk; Cathy took the filing cabinet.

The surface of the desk was extremely clean. On a blotter lay a letter opener, an ornate inkpot of black-painted wrought iron, and three pens. A small calendar lay to the right, next to the lamp.

Unusually clean, and Keel couldn't even see a coffee stain on the polished desk surface. The blotting paper itself had no marks on it. The unused look of the desk should have told Keel to watch out, but it didn't register.

He tried the main drawer in the center. It contained paper clips, a selection of rubber bands, and other normal desk items. The top right drawer contained blank sheets of paper, and envelopes bearing the Knight Industries logo and address. The second drawer down was locked. Using the letter opener, Keel worked the lock free and opened the drawer. It contained small plastic cards, all identical to the one that had gained them entry. Keel was about to shut the drawer when he had a second thought. He pocketed several of the cards, just in case. You never knew what might come in useful in this game.

He turned to try the top left-hand drawer, and then froze. There was a thin letter-box slit cut into the woodwork, barely a centimeter below the lip of the desktop. It was almost unnoticeable, in fact. It reminded him of the card slot outside. Thoughtfully, he tried one of the cards he had just taken from the drawer in this hole.

There was a slight whine, and then the card moved toward him. He backed away as he realized that it wasn't the card, but the whole front of the desk. A hidden shelf was emerging. It formed a small ledge about two feet square. On top of it was a map that he recognized instantly.

Katawa . . .

He examined it with care, noting that it showed several significant red-marked spots. Each was just over the border inside the country. Two were small villages, and one was a town. The final three seemed to be nothing at all, but all had significance, clearly. Bases of some sort? Shipping points? The names rang a bell in the back of his mind. He almost had it when Cathy called softly to him.

"Keel!" She had the filing cabinet open and was rummaging through the hanging files inside it. Keel took a last look at the map and moved to join her.

She held a file marked "Keller." It had been stamped in red—TERMINATED—and held a photo of a young man. Cathy looked grim. "Someone who got too close, it seems." She gestured toward the drawer. "There's another of these, too, a man called Harrison."

"It fits the pattern," Keel said, just as quietly. "I'd have been surprised if whoever was behind this would concern himself too much about the spilling of blood. Anything else?"

Cathy took the next file from the pile she held in her hand. She handed it to him. It had one word on the cover: KEEL.

Opening it, he found a picture of his own face staring back at him. Behind this was a sheet of paper that listed all of his salient features, his address, and his habits. At the bottom, added later in a different typeface, was Cowles's address and the date both of them were due to leave for Katawa. It confirmed that the mastermind behind this had laid the trail carefully—Keel had been intended to witness the kidnapping of Cowles.

Closing the file, he asked: "Is there one for you?"

Wordlessly, Cathy handed him a second file. It, too, contained a picture and a description of her habits. Added in this one was a clipping about the gorilla. "Sure to interest her," someone had scrawled across the top in red ink.

"Just as a wild guess," Keel whispered. "How about Steed?"

Cathy didn't hand him a file this time. Instead, she opened the second drawer. "Steed, in all his glory," she explained. "The entire contents refer to him."

Restraining the impulse to whistle, Keel grunted instead. "He's popular, isn't he?" he whispered, flicking through the files.

"It's not just information about Steed," Cathy said coldly. "It's a recipe on how to *make* Steed."

"Make him? I don't follow you. Make him do what?"

Cathy drew out a small set of blueprints and showed them to him. Electronics wasn't his field, but he could see that they were circuit diagrams. Very sophisticated, too. And a long list of parameters. "I get it—they're trying to make Steed break the bank at Monte Carlo, and this little contraption will help him beat the roulette wheel."

Almost as wild as the truth. Sighing, Cathy informed him: "Given the right equipment to build one, you could make a robot of Steed from that information."

"Not *could*, my dear Mrs. Gale," said a new voice cheerfully. "Did."

They both spun about, only to see a pistol trained in their direction. Above the pistol, his eyes twinkling with amusement at Keel's reaction, was Dr. Bennett Cowles.

"My dear David," he murmured as if surprised. "How good to see you again, old chap." The gun in his hand made it clear that he expected the pleasure of their visit to be extended.

A wave of anger swept over Keel as he realized what a fool he'd been. "The kidnapping was a fake," he snarled.

Cowles smiled. "But very cleverly executed, you must admit. You see, I hired—ah, Marty and his friends. I asked them to kidnap a Dr. Cowles and bring him here. I simply neglected to mention that *I* was Cowles. That way, they thought the whole thing was for real."

"Why?" Keel spat the word like venom.

"Because our trip to Katawa was brought forward, my dear chap," Cowles replied. "I simply can't afford to leave for at least another week yet. By then, everything will be ready. So I simply had to vanish convincingly for a while. In seven days' time, certain friends of mine will be contacted, a ransom arranged, and then I shall be released. The police will simply assume that the whole thing was for the money. I may even give them a good description of Marty and his friends, just to add to the authenticity."

It was all beginning to add up now for Keel. A picture of what had occurred flashed across his mind. "You knew I'd find Marty and his pals and thump this address from him."

"Of course. I selected Marty mainly because of his wonderful talent of cracking under pressure. That's why I had him bring me here—safe in the knowledge that you'd be along very shortly."

"And me?" asked Cathy casually.

"You, Mrs. Gale, were pure happenstance. I'd planned to have you here, of course, but a trifle later on. The gorilla business was a pure fluke."

Keel's eyes narrowed. "And what happens now?"

"My dear chap, I really do have need of you. Just not as you presently are, that's all." Cowles's smile never wavered, nor did the gun. "I see I came in just a moment or two too soon—but I simply couldn't resist a dramatic entrance. Mrs. Gale, if you'd be so kind, please open the third drawer down."

Cathy shrugged and did as directed. Inside the drawer were two large envelopes. One had her name on it, the other had Keel's. Cowles smiled and gestured her to proceed. She opened hers, and inside it were more schematics and specifications. "Robots," she breathed.

"Not quite," Cowles corrected. He gestured slightly, and two more figures entered the room. Both were tall, bulky beings, and each wore a large, belted raincoat and snap-brimmed hat. Each had thick black gloves on. Each had a gray metallic face, permanently frozen in a steel stare. Cowles smiled again. "Cybernauts," he said.

13 Avenging Angels

As Steed turned the Bentley's nose into Swain's Lane, Emma could see the spire of St. Michael's church to their right. It was barely visible in the thickening gloom as night fell about them. Steed drew up to the entrance to the new area of the cemetery and cut the engine.

"Fancy a walk?" he asked lightly.

Emma reflected on a serious answer. Would she like to wander through a graveyard at night looking for the tomb of an apparently deceased mad scientist? Then she smiled back: "It's too late for our picnic."

"If we're done fast enough," Steed told her, "we could always nip into The Flask for a cheese sandwich and the best pint in the area."

"I'll bear that in mind." She joined Steed at the

entrance to the cemetery. The gate was locked, but such a minor problem had never bothered Steed in the past. Nor did it now; he had it open in a couple of seconds.

He held the gate. "After you," he offered politely.

Emma looked at the dark stones and shadowy trees beyond. She didn't believe in ghosts, but in this line of business, she had run across some *very* weird things. "Lead on," she replied. Doffing his bowler, Steed nodded and set off at a brisk pace. She stuck close behind him, not wanting him to get too far ahead. It would be difficult to find him again. The thought almost amused her: Steed, lost forever in a graveyard. "Steed? What do we do when we get to the tomb?"

"We make sure Armstrong's not gone walkies," he called back over his shoulder, twirling his ever-present umbrella.

"And how do we do that? Dig up the body?"

"No need. There's a family crypt, and I brought along my, ah, skeleton key."

Trust Steed to make light of descending into a family tomb to look for a body at night!

"Do you think he'll be still there?" Emma glanced about, not exactly nervously—more *alertly*, she hoped. Just in case they were jumped. She didn't try to envisage what might jump them.

"I do hope so," said Steed. "I'd hate to try to track down the body. Not really my line of work."

Emma bit back the temptation to point out that *her* line of work happened to be manufacturing, not staking out the undead. Instead, she focused her eyes on the small of Steed's back and wished she had a knife . . .

"Ah!" he said after a few more minutes. "Here we are: the Armstrong crypt!" He sounded like Sir Richard Burton discovering the source of the Nile.

The crypt was an old one, obviously dating back to the previous century. It was about twenty feet high, and as many wide and long. The main portion was of some dark stone, weathered and a little chipped. The Armstrong name had been chiseled into the front. Below it was an entryway that was partially sunk into the ground. Three steps led down to its huge oak door, and a large and rusty-looking padlock hung through the bolt. The only thing that made this tomb stand out from the others was the rococo effect created by four large stone angels, one at each corner of the crypt. Their wings spread, they were obviously the pillars holding up the roof. In the dim light of a far-off street lamp, they looked more demonic than angelic to Emma.

Steed skipped down the steps and examined the padlock. "Not a very efficient way to keep visitors out—or ghosties in." He started to play with it, easing the point of his umbrella between the links of the chain. After a moment, Emma heard a rusty creak. Steed pulled at the chain, and the whole lock came free in his hand. He casually tossed it aside. Then he pushed gently at the door. It opened silently.

"Curious," Emma remarked. "A rusty lock, but an oiled door." She pulled a small flashlight from one of her pockets and turned it on. The narrow beam probed the darkness, casting shadows onto the walls. "Won't you walk into my parlor . . . ?"

"Why not?" Steed asked. She noticed that his perpetual grin had vanished now. It seemed to be due less to nervousness than to anticipation. Steed vanished through the doorway, and she had no choice but to follow.

The interior of the crypt was a few feet lower than the ground outside, and smelled dank. The earth seemed to press about them in the room. Around three of the walls were low stone plinths. On them lay coffins. The center of the crypt was clear, and a single thick stone pillar supported the roof.

"No dust," Emma commented, running her finger along a casket.

"They must be homebodies," Steed joked. He bent to examine the small plaque below the first coffin. "Sir Arthur Armstrong. Died 1921." The next. "Lady Cornelia Armstrong. Died 1923." He straightened up, removing a flashlight from his own pocket—an industrial one with a powerful beam. "Why don't you try the far wall? It'll be quicker that way." He started to probe about with his bright beam.

"Scared?" she mocked.

"Hungry," he corrected. "That cheese sandwich is calling my name." He bent back to study the next plaque. Emma grinned in the gloom and did as he suggested.

The Armstrongs were obviously either a large family or this tomb went back farther than she had at first supposed. There were at least twenty coffins in this single room, in various stages of decomposition. Presumably, though, Armstrong's own coffin would be relatively fresh.

The beam from her small torch cut a white swath through the gloom and picked out a single coffin away from all the others. It was worth a try, so she bent to read the inscription. "Uncle Evelyn Armstrong," she mused aloud.

"Uncle Evelyn!" Steed exclaimed. "So they had one, too."

"So?" Emma asked, unable to understand his apparent animation. "We all have uncles, Steed. And from the way that this coffin is placed, I'd guess he was the black sheep of the family."

"Mine, too," Steed replied mysteriously. "Remind me to tell you about her sometime."

"*Her?*" Emma asked. "*Uncle* Evelyn."

"A relative scoundrel. Made my life hell." It was clear that Steed was enjoying perplexing her. Emma often wondered if his family was as extensive and eccentric as he always claimed. Still, it would take a pretty unusual family to produce an offspring like him.

"Ah!" she exclaimed, playing her beam over another coffin.

This was one set slightly apart from the rest, at the back of the crypt. She crossed to it and shone her light on the top of the casket. DR. HENRY ARMSTRONG. BORN 1921. There was no date of death on the lid. Fighting back the chills, she called Steed over. Her voice was lower than she had expected, and she tried to convince herself that this was nonsense. Armstrong was dead, and the missing date was simply an oversight.

Or deliberate, some inner devil whispered.

Steed joined her and looked at the inscription. "That's our man," he murmured. "Let's just check he's not popped out for a cheese sandwich, shall we?"

He tried the lid of the casket. It was made of mahogany and refused to budge. There was a small headpiece. Carefully, Steed prised at this with the tip of his umbrella. It suddenly swung open and stayed in a vertical position. The beam from his flashlight glinted on what lay within.

It was neither a face nor a skull. Instead, it was a metallic plate. They looked at one another in mute puzzlement; the plate looked ominously like the face mask of a Cybernaut. Yet the features were undoubtedly those of Armstrong—gaunt and savage.

"Is there a body?" Emma asked. Her voice was terribly close to a whisper.

Steed shone the light under the lid into the rest of the coffin. "Yes," he confirmed.

Emma realized she had been holding her breath. She let it out in one long burst.

If Steed noticed, he didn't comment. Instead, he gestured at the death mask. "I suppose they had to do that—Armstrong was battered up pretty badly during the fight with the Cybernaut that killed him."

Emma nodded, finding it difficult to take her eyes from the perfectly accurate features on the mask. It looked as though Armstrong's flesh had been transformed into metal, which lay there, waiting for—

Metal eyelids opened, and two intense glowing-red eyes were revealed. The head turned slightly in the coffin to look at them. The mouth opened slightly. "Ah!" a metallic voice breathed.

"Steed—and Mrs. Peel. Come to make sure that I'm really dead?"

Emma felt cold now. The demonic eyes seemed to bore into her soul, and the prickle of the supernatural seeped through the place. Even Steed looked paler, and his smile had been dashed away. Or was it merely a trick of the light?

"Rest assured," Armstrong's voice whispered to them. "I am indeed deceased. But that will not stop me. The body may perish, but Science still lives. And with the powers we can harness from the natural forces of the universe—can anything stay dead forever? Steed, Mrs. Peel—I may be dead, but I shall still have my retribution. Together, you have destroyed what I dreamed into existence—but I am not alone in my visions. There are others. And there are angels of death at my command. Steed, Mrs. Peel—the death knell has been rung for you both. You will perish, and you will know that it is by my hand."

"My, he goes on a bit," Steed muttered. He reached into the coffin and groped about for a moment. Then the burning eyes went dead and Steed fished out a small tape recorder. "Activated when the lid is opened," he confirmed. "It looks as though we were expected."

The prosaic truth of the "haunting" sent Emma's adrenaline surging again. She watched almost giddily as Steed rewound the tape and started it again. "Ah!" said the hollow voice once again. "Steed—and Mrs. Peel!" He clicked it off.

"Curious," he said. "Unless this has been there for some time—and I doubt it, considering the lock on the door—then whoever planted it must have known that we were working together again. Which means the message must have been freshly recorded."

"Or perhaps they meant us to be working together again," Emma suggested. "Perhaps the taped message purporting to be from Mother was the bait to bring you back to me and to get us active again. And this taped message must have been made on the same voice synthesizer that made the earlier recording."

"Undoubtedly." Steed replaced the recorder in the coffin and closed the lid. "We're on the right track, clearly. But whoever is behind all of this is staying at least one step ahead of us."

"Why do I get the feeling that we'll be expected at my factory in Crawley?"

He grinned again, that infectious, devil-may-care smile that signaled the quarry in sight. "Because we undoubtedly will be. So let's not keep our host waiting any longer, shall we? He may have some even more theatrical props to help us on our way otherwise."

Emma nodded and started back to the world outside the crypt. "But what I still don't understand," she called over her shoulder, "is why this link with Armstrong?"

"According to the tape, he had help when he was working on the Cybernauts. Armstrong was a genius, without a doubt, but even he couldn't do everything himself. At a guess, I'd say he had a protégé who takes particular exception to the fact that we killed Armstrong and wants us to know that his revenge is for that act."

Pausing while Steed locked the door, Emma

thought about this. "But *we* didn't kill him; his own inventions did."

He grinned. "I don't think that will make much difference to the raving nutcase behind this affair. We do seem to find them, don't we?"

"And the bit about angels to avenge him?"

Steed shrugged. "Perhaps thoughts of divine retribution?"

There was a slight grating sound, as if some metallic cover was being slowly moved back. Emma spun around, looking back at the crypt. "Or some more immediate form," she muttered, pointing.

The angel at the left edge of the tomb had turned its face to look at them. Twin red eyes—matching those of the artificial head of Armstrong—burned out of the darkness at them. There was another of the creaks, and the two huge wings slowly uncurled from the stone. In a series of metallic groans, the angel prised itself free of the vault. The stonelike appearance of the statue clearly covered another of the sophisticated robots they had already encountered.

Then the second angel started to move, followed by the final two from the rear of the tomb. Each dragged itself free of the crypt and moved to join the first one.

Emma risked a glance at Steed, who was holding his umbrella like a sword and watching the apparitions carefully. She started to inch backward, wondering what would happen next. Would these robotic cherubs spring for them?

Instead, the ground shook slightly. Twin jets of flame shot from the feet of each of the figures. The angels slowly rose from the ground, arms moving upward, wings outspread as though to catch a non-existent wind. Then, like rockets, the four figures shot into the air.

"Most impressive," commented Steed. "He even makes them fly."

"Let's get back to the car," Emma suggested, worried. She doubted that flying away was all that they had been programmed to do.

"A splendid idea," Steed enthused. "Last one back to the Bentley is a rotten egg." He sprinted down the path. Emma followed him, glancing back as she ran.

There was a scream of something rushing through the air, and then a staccato burst of noise. Bullets ripped into the grass and graves beside them. Emma threw herself into a roll, knocking aside an urn of freshly potted roses. She then dove for cover behind a headstone.

The angel pulled out of the dive, flashing about ten feet over her head. It caught the light just enough for her to see that two machine guns had appeared in openings in the shoulders, just in front of the wings. Then the flying machine was gone.

She could see Steed, similarly crouched behind a headstone. He was holding his bowler hat in place. As she looked, he poked a finger through a hole in the brim. The attack had been closer than she had thought. "The angels of death, indeed," she murmured to herself.

There was another whine and the second angel shot out of the darkness, heading for her. Its machine guns opened fire, and Emma heard the bullets zinging off the stone that shielded her. The angel passed overhead, and something fell from it.

Emma dived, rolled, and came to her feet, running in one fluid movement. Behind her, something hit the grave she had been resting on. It exploded in flames, knocking her from her feet again. As the dust, earth, and granite chippings settled, Steed materialized beside her.

"They're making enough noise to wake the dead," he complained.

"I think their target is the living," Emma pointed out. "I'll meet you back at the Bentley. If we split up, that'll give them two targets to try for. It may confuse them."

Steed nodded and slid off into the darkness. He was taking a zigzag pattern through the plots—a longer route, but potentially safer. Emma removed thoughts of him from her conscious mind and set about taking a different path back to the gatehouse.

There was another of the now-familiar whines, and she dodged behind a tree. It shook as bullets slammed into it, gouging holes into the trunk. Something seared a path of sticky pain across her left shoulder. She clamped her hand to it, feeling blood. Then the angel was gone again and silence returned. She started off once more, keeping away from the paths and not worrying about how many urns she kicked over in the dark.

A sharp explosion and a plume of fire about a hundred feet away told her that an angel had attacked Steed. She simply had to believe that he'd escaped the blast, and she continued on her way.

She ran again, stumbling, wishing that there were more lights—or would that only help their attackers? Another whine ahead alerted her. "Angels at twelve o'clock high," she muttered. Throwing herself to one side, she evaded the pass. Bullets whacked into the ground behind her, and she straightened up.

Right in the path of another angel. This one had her dead in sight. There was simply no way it could miss her. Desperately, Emma threw herself forward, expecting to feel the bullets cutting into her as she hit the ground.

Instead, the earth opened up beneath her and she plunged forward into darkness. The bullets slammed into the spot where she should have been. Emma crunched into the ground at the bottom of a pit, winded but very much alive. Shaking her head, she straightened up, disentangling herself from a sheet of rubber.

She'd stumbled onto a freshly dug grave! It had been covered to keep the rain out, ready for a burial. In the darkness, the rubber tarpaulin had looked just like the dark ground. There couldn't be many people who could say that ending up in the grave had saved their lives . . .

She gripped the edge of the hole and levered herself up to peer over the edge. The angel had passed over but would most definitely be back. By the side of the grave, Emma saw the spade that had been left there. It was very long-handled, and an idea formed in her mind. Risky, but she had nothing to lose . . .

Pulling herself out of the grave, she clutched the shovel to her, then set off again for the exit. The pain in her injured shoulder was intense, but she pushed it away for the moment. Her ears were waiting to hear the whine of the rockets powering the killer robots. She ignored the occasional bruises as she slammed into gravestones, markers, or pots of flowers. Finally—probably only a minute later—she heard the sound of an approaching angel. Quickly, she ducked behind the largest tombstone in the vicinity and listened.

The roar came louder, and she forced herself to hold steady. Then, praying for good luck, she sprang out, whipping the spade over her head.

The angel was too close to hit her now, the guns in its shoulders unable to depress far enough. The robot slammed into the spade's head, and the tool, smacking hard, spun from Emma's grip. As she had hoped, though, the blow had done its work. Part of the monstrous face had been dented in and sparks flew across the stony cheek. The rockets wavered and the angel started to wobble in the air. Then, like a stricken aircraft, it plunged to the earth. Hitting the pathway, it exploded, showering metal, stone, and gravel all about. In the glare of the licking flames, Emma could see her way much better. Passing the burning wreckage, she murmured: "Rest in pieces."

She was only about twenty feet from the gateway when the flames caught what was left of the rocket fuel. The resulting blast knocked her from her feet, throwing her into the side of a grass verge. The blow stunned her, and she tried vainly to regain her feet. Through hazy vision, she could see another of the angels swooping down from the night sky to open fire on her.

Then Steed materialized beside her. In his arms he cradled the rocket launcher he had used to destroy the submarine. "Bless the Boy Scouts," Emma said weakly. Steed grinned, and fired.

The angel went to glory in one huge explosion that lit the sky like day. Metallic rubble rained down on them, sizzling as each piece hit the grass. Steed grinned. "Two down, two to go."

"I hope you've got more ammunition for that thing," Emma said, finally able to get to her feet. "Otherwise, it's our wings that'll get clipped."

"That's all," Steed told her sadly. "I've used up the entire box."

"Any good ideas?"

"Yes. Run!" Together they sprinted for the gatehouse again. They could see Steed's Bentley waiting in the road as the final two angels screamed down out of the sky at them.

They were caught out in the open. Too far from the gate to use its arched columns and wall as a shield, they were also too far from the nearest graves for any protection that they might offer. There was only one thing they could do, and they did it, diving away from one another while running as fast as they could.

There was a single gunshot, but nothing hit Emma. Puzzled, she glanced back over her shoulder.

Tara King stood in the gateway, a huge Magnum pistol clenched in both fists. Taking careful aim, she fired again. This time she hit the lead angel. Trailing smoke, it spun out of the sky and crashed into the ground. Tara's third shot sent the final angel reeling, and she added two more bullets to be certain. That angel didn't even make it to the ground; it detonated in the air as a bullet hit the fuel tank.

Emma brushed the hair from her eyes, suddenly

aware that sweat was plastering the long locks to her head. Had she been that terrified? Yes, she realized as her body finally managed to come down from its adrenaline high. She had not expected to survive the attack. On unsteady legs, she walked over to where Tara was calmly reloading her oversized gun.

Steed reached her first, a big smile on his face. "Tara!" he exclaimed. "You're an . . . angel."

She smiled sweetly, then glanced at Emma. "Mrs. Peel, you've been wounded."

Emma had almost forgotten about that; now she could allow herself the luxury of the pain. "I'm sure it's just a graze," she said. Tara nodded, but took a closer look. Then she reached into her voluminous bag and pulled out a small, sterile dressing. Emma looked on as Tara expertly applied it.

"I seem to have arrived at the right time," Tara commented.

"Thankfully, yes," Steed agreed. "But what brought you here?"

"You did," Tara replied. "Or rather, a very good facsimile of you. I managed to dispense with it, Steed, but not before it had drastically rearranged your living room. You now have through ventilation."

"Fresh air is good for one," Steed said, realizing that Tara was worried about his reaction. Apartments could be fixed; dead friends could not. "It was *me*, you say?"

"Exactly like you."

"Not quite, Tara. *I* would have killed you."

"I recalled what you had told me about those

two fights you had with the Cybernauts, and I did some checking. Which led me here."

"In time to prevent myself and Mrs. Peel from taking up permanent residence," Steed concluded. He linked his arm through Tara's as she replaced the pistol in her huge handbag. Emma wondered what else lurked inside that monstrosity. Steed then took her arm as well, placing himself between them, and marched them back toward the waiting Bentley.

As they reached it, a policeman drew up on his bicycle, pedaling furiously. He seemed very cross and red-faced as he flopped the bike onto the cemetery wall. Puffing from his exertions, he walked over to them.

"Good evening, Officer," Steed greeted him cheerfully.

"Maybe for some, sir," said the bobby doubtfully. He had his truncheon in his hand, clearly prepared for trouble, but Steed—as always—looked impeccably the gentleman, and the last person in the world to be breaking the law. "The station's had reports of someone shooting off fireworks hereabouts."

"Fireworks?" Steed echoed, as though astonished. "Goodness, is it November the Fifth already?"

"No, sir, it isn't," the policeman said patiently. "It's not even close." He looked from Steed to Tara—who had assumed an air of cultured bewilderment—to Emma, whose cat suit was torn. He frowned as he saw the dressing on her shoulder where the bullet had opened the skin. "May I inquire as to what you were doing in the cemetery at this time of night?"

"Paying our last respects to a late, unlamented acquaintance," Steed told him. "At least, I sincerely hope that they were last respects." The strain seemed to finally have told on him. The two women could see a haunted look in his eyes. "But I have a strong suspicion that this long night is not over yet."

"Come again?" the policeman asked, baffled.

"If I do come again," Steed informed him, "it will be inside a casket, ready to join the illustrious other Steeds within the family crypt." He doffed his hat politely. "Good evening. I do hope you nab the culprits." Glancing over his shoulder, he couldn't resist adding: "Good grief—I do believe they've lit a bonfire!"

"What?" The policeman followed his gaze, his face falling. "Lummee, you're right, sir!" He started for the flickering light he could see. When he glanced back, the Bentley and the three people were gone.

14 Just Another Tomorrow-the-World Maniac After All

Cowles seemed to be enjoying his sense of power tremendously. He had taken the seat behind the desk, settling comfortably into the plush leather, and swung it to face them. He had replaced the gun in his pocket, but neither Keel nor Cathy could try to overpower him. The two Cybernauts held their arms firmly in powerful, metallic grips. Keel's gun had been taken from him; one of the Cybernauts had impassively crushed it in its steel grip and then allowed the broken metal to fall to the floor.

"It really is quite a pleasure to have you here, you know, Keel," Cowles said, linking his fingers over his stomach. "This is the culmination of years of work."

Keel glared at him. "I don't understand. You're a man of power and wealth, respected and—I thought—a friend. So what's the story with this factory and these metal monsters?"

"A friend?" Cowles laughed long and hard. Finally, wiping away tears from his eyes, he shook his head. "My dear Keel, you were never that! You were always a target, a victim-to-be. It's simply that over the years I have gotten very good with my public image. I played the fool for you—all that altruism that you sincerely believed in! All that drivel about helping the unfortunate souls! You weak, stupid cretin—all those lofty ideals that you believed in but which I despise!" For the first time, Cowles's implacable good humor slipped, and Keel could see a terrible depth of hatred in his burning eyes.

"Why?" he asked simply.

"Why?" Cowles leaped to his feet, his face reddening. "Why, you ask me?" He looked as though he was ready to storm around the desk and hit Keel. After a moment, though, he managed to fight down this inner fury and he calmed down, almost back to the jovial façade that Keel was so used to. "Let me tell you a story," he finally said, settling back into the chair. He looked up at the ceiling thoughtfully.

"Before the War, I was not Cowles. My real name is no longer of any significance, but I lived in Berlin, was a physician of note and respect there. I was in good standing with the Nazi Party, and my research was in genetics. My work came to the attention of the Führer, who allowed me considerable liberties to conduct my experiments. As the War progressed, I began to discover many interesting things. Watson and Crick's discovery of the double helix in genetic material in 1953 was not the first time that a scientist found out about the mechanism of the transmission of genetic data. *I* was ten years ahead of them, working in Berlin. Needless to say, I could not publish, and after the War, I could not tell anyone what I knew. The moral climate at that time would not have approved of the method by which I had gained my data.

"I went farther, much farther, than Watson and Crick. I discovered the secrets of DNA and RNA long before their paper was published. I found a way to make a person's genes replicate in the laboratory, and discovered chemicals within the living brain that contained RNA, encoded with the memory. I found that I could take these extracts from cerebrospinal fluids from one individual and inject them into another person. The memories of the first person could thus be passed along to another.

"The one unsolvable problem for me was that the second person's personality would suppress the thoughts of the first, and eventually the RNA memories would break down. I had been looking for a way, you see, of keeping a person alive by transmitting his memories into a host body. We are, after all, no more than the sum of our memories. My theory was that if I could somehow encapsulate the memories of a person and then transfer those memories intact to a second mind, I could thus recreate the first person.

"I attempted everything that I could think of to make the transfer permanent, but to no avail. Most subjects simply . . . died. Clearly, then, that line of thought was a dead end. So I began another series of experiments—if I could take a person's genes and somehow replicate that person, then perhaps I could manage what I was after. Nowadays the term, I believe, is 'cloning.' I began to attempt this, but before I could complete my experiments, the War was over and Germany was falling. I had to escape with my knowledge, somehow, and begin anew.

"I fled Berlin before the Russians arrived, taking refuge where I could. Finally, I stumbled across a man who was dying, injured in the shelling of Berlin. It was an English doctor, attached to the Army Medical Corps. His name, as you may have guessed, was Cowles. I killed him and took over his identity, deliberately injuring myself badly enough to be mistaken for him. I was found and shipped home—home!—to England for recovery.

"So I *became* Cowles. Fortune blessed my every move. He was an orphan, and so I could slip easily into his life. I was careful to pretend that I had had a concussion, explaining my apparent memory loss for friends and details. Gradually these kindly fools 'refreshed' my memories and helped me to become Cowles. I was a successful surgeon, hiding my true feelings for the work I was doing, playing the part of the philanthropist. All the time, I worked on my experiments in secret, growing DNA chains, and finally I managed to perform the miracle that I had been seeking—growing a living body from genetic material taken from another person."

Keel could hardly believe his ears. He didn't *want* to believe it. Cathy struggled in the Cybernaut's grasp, trying to free herself. She winced in pain as the metallic hands simply closed tighter.

"You're wasting your time, Mrs. Gale." Cowles smiled. "It will never release its hold, unless I order it to. Now, where was I? Oh, yes . . . this was six years ago. Then I was contacted by a group who knew my real identity—an organization named Eisenhand." He smiled as he saw Keel's reaction to the name. "Ah, I believe that I have touched a nerve there, haven't I?"

Memory came flooding back to Keel. "Steed and I destroyed Eisenhand several years ago." He glanced at Cathy and explained: "Eisenhand was a group of ex-Nazis who wanted to set up a new Reich here in this country. A man called Drucker—Klaus Drucker—was behind it. They had the help of a scientist named Jaeger, who had surgically altered escaped war criminals who were reported dead. Steed and I destroyed the group. Drucker and Jaeger were both killed."

"Murdered," Cowles snarled, his mask slipping again. "They were murdered by you and Steed. You were trying to stop them, and to avoid a trial and publicity for their cause—and public sympathy for their aims—you murdered them both."

Angry, Keel snapped back: "That's a lie! We did not kill either of them. They died—"

"Call it what you will!" howled Cowles. "Both men died as a result of your intervention. My friend, and my brother."

With sudden understanding, Keel stared at the man he thought he had known. "You were part of Eisenhand, then. Part of that plot to take over England."

"Never," Cowles answered. He had managed once again to regain something of his composure and self-control. His volatile moods were unsettling, but years of masking his true feelings had given him a tight rein on his temper. "Jaeger and I were old colleagues, and my brother Klaus and I—we were always close. But I thought that their plan was doomed to failure. They believed that this country was ripe for the rebirth of the ideals of Germany. This is a shiftless, soulless age, and it needs a strong philosophy to give it meaning. But this country is not yet ready for a takeover. There is not enough dissatisfaction with the government, not enough social problems. I told them to try elsewhere, but they would not heed my advice. And now they are both dead." He stared at Keel, hatred in his features. "I vowed then to get my revenge, but I knew it would take time. I am a patient man, Keel—I have been forced to be by the nature of my work. Each step took me years to perfect. Each advance would take a decade to prove its worth. So I waited, and kept track of your movements.

"Then, finally, it all came together. After all these years, I am gaining what I wanted in one simple movement—thanks to that stupid fool M'Begwe!"

Cathy, fascinated and appalled in equal measure, interjected: "Then this connection with Katawa is no coincidence?"

Cowles sneered. "Of course not. I managed to use my influence in this matter. It was at my suggestion that M'Begwe used the gorilla park to bring you in. It was at my suggestion that the W.H.O. decided to send Keel to Katawa. I planned then to join him there."

Keel grunted, seeing how Cowles had neatly

planned each move. "Then your only piece of luck was the plague."

His face open and guileless, Cowles raised an eyebrow. "Luck?" he echoed. "I don't believe in luck, Keel. I *create* it."

The full import of his words almost made Keel's blood boil. He stared at the other man in disgust. "You did it," he breathed. "You *created* that plague. That's why it's so specific—you tailored it just to attack the Katawans!" Memory of the map in the desk came back. "The positions on your map—the sites of the plague."

Cowles smiled at the naked hatred being thrown his way. "I knew that you would finally catch on," he said modestly. "As I mentioned, I have been planning this takeover for more than a decade. I could not wait for a natural problem to call me into my chosen site. I told Klaus he needed a base of power that was much simpler to take over than England. A place where the inhabitants could be defeated by deceit and technology. A place to establish a forward base. But Klaus was too impatient. Unlike me, he could not wait a decade to see the results of his planning. He wanted everything today. That was his failing, and that eventually led to his murder. But I—I am content to start small and then build from that power base."

Cathy stared at him in disgust. "You're just another of those tomorrow-the-world maniacs," she sneered. "You aim to somehow take over Katawa and then use it as a springboard for the rest of the world?"

"Don't dare take that tone with me!" Cowles screamed. "I could order those metal arms to close tighter and tighter till they crushed the life out of you!"

"But you won't," Keel said hastily, in case he followed through on that threat. "At least not yet, will you? You have something else in mind." He desperately hoped that he was correct in this belief, and that Cathy would not be murdered at that very instant.

Getting a grip on his fury again, Cowles calmed down. "No," he agreed. "Not yet. It would be too soon for that pleasure." He turned to Cathy. "As you surmise, though, I do indeed plan to take over Katawa. I have been experimenting with a partner on the perfect way to do just that. He provided me with the raw tool—the Cybernauts."

Although Keel and Cathy were both unfamiliar with these creations, they could tell that they were a powerful weapon. Mindless, lacking any ethical qualms, they could be the perfect killing machines. An army of Cybernauts, all marching at Cowles's command. Keel saw mirrored in Cathy's expression his own feelings of horror.

Cowles laughed at their reaction. "Ah, you are thinking of those Cybernauts that hold you immobile!" He clambered to his feet. "Impressive, are they not? A soulless army, one that will give even truer meaning to the word 'blitzkrieg' when they are turned loose! But they are simply the rank and file, the new foot soldiers for the Reich that I am planning. They will fight and crush all opposition, truly, but they are not all that I have. If I were to invade Katawa with them, then the world would turn against me." He slapped the arm of the robot holding Cathy. "Wonderful as they are, there are not yet enough of them to form the army that I would require for such a task. I need the resources of Katawa to build that army. In the meantime, there is a much better way of taking power."

He walked to the door. "Follow me," he ordered. Keel couldn't tell whether he was addressing him and Cathy or the Cybernauts, but it made no practical difference. The robots began to move, and their prisoners were forced to walk. Cowles, obviously very pleased with himself, took them out of the office and through the main floor of the factory. The machinery lay silent, with only occasional lights illuminating the room. On the far side was a door with another of the card slots. Cowles took one of the plastic cards from his pocket and inserted it into the slot. The door hissed open, and he led them through.

Inside, the room was lined with rows of metal lockers. It reminded Keel of nothing so much as the morgue. He watched as Cowles unfastened one door and swung it open. Inside was a still form, laid out on a metal table. Cowles pulled the shelf out and displayed the "body" with a flourish. "Allow me to introduce you to the next generation of Cybernauts!" he announced. "Not merely faceless beings, but androids, replicas of living people." Grinning with pleasure, he stepped back to allow his captives a better view.

Keel and Cathy both looked down at a face that they knew only too well: the firm, hard features, the dark skin, the grizzled hair. It was a Cybernaut in the likeness of Prime Minister M'Begwe of Katawa.

15 Haven't I Seen Me Somewhere Before?

In the backseat of the Bentley, Emma examined the voice synthesizer with interest. "So this is how it's done?"

Tara, firmly entrenched at Steed's side as he drove, leaned back and nodded. "You program the tone and mannerisms via that small bank of controls, and then you use the keys to make separate sounds, which are recorded on that small tape deck. Once you are finished with the recording, then you simply play it back. Presto, it can sound like anyone you want."

"How very ingenious of Professor Lipp," Emma approved.

"Yes," Tara agreed. "He saw a lot of good uses for it. Unfortunately for him, his partner had other things in mind."

"I can see it now." Steed sighed, carefully steering his way through the dark lanes, heading for Crawley. "Politicians would love one of those. Just record a speech and then play it through that—one could make it sound like Winston Churchill. Might get them a lot more votes."

"I thought you always slept through political speeches," Emma remarked. "Anyway, you could use it for translation—have someone translate your speech into a language you don't know, then play it back on this in your own voice to impress the natives."

"Or you could do what our unknown mastermind has done and use it to frame someone," Tara pointed out.

"Quite," Steed agreed. "Thankfully, neither you nor I were really fooled for a minute." He caught Emma's reproachful look in the rearview mirror. "At most, for a few fleeting seconds," he corrected himself.

Tara sighed. "Now what?" she asked. "This device was built at your factory in Crawley," she commented to Emma. "And it's a safe bet that that's where these new Cybernauts were made, as well as the copies of Steed and Rhonda. But *why*?"

"I'm confident that at least some of this is personal business," Emma said thoughtfully. "It's been designed to draw both Steed and myself into the game. That message at Armstrong's tomb suggests that whoever is behind this has a grudge with us both, probably connected to Armstrong himself."

"Quite right, Mrs. Peel," Steed agreed. "And the resurgence of the Cybernauts is an alarming event. I thought they were well out of the way. It wasn't a simple job to dispose of them before. And this new bunch appears to be a far more sophisticated lot and infinitely more difficult to detect. As Tara has proven."

Emma nodded, recalling their previous two encounters with the killer robots. "The older Cybernauts weren't really autonomous," she observed. "They needed a target to lock in on. They used those pen devices that Armstrong built to locate their prey. Those angels of death didn't have an electronic homer, did they?"

"I never thought to frisk them," Steed answered.

"And the replica of you," Tara interjected, "seemed . . . well, almost *alive*. Intelligent. It responded to my conversation, and to my movements."

"Some kind of internal brain," Emma suggested.

"A little computer in their heads?" Steed questioned.

"Possibly," Emma concurred. "But it would have to be tremendously complex in design."

"Ah!" breathed Steed. "Then there's our chance. The more complicated a thing is, the simpler it is to break down. All those newfangled inventions they get us to buy nowadays—they break down so easily."

"That's because you mistreat them," Emma commented.

"Be that as it may," Steed replied cheerfully, "all we have to do is to discover in these new Cybernauts a weakness . . ."

There was silence for a few moments, each lost in thought. Then Emma tapped Tara's shoulder. "You mentioned that you knocked out the duplicate of Steed, but how?"

"I helped it out of a window."

"Then all we have to do," Steed suggested, "is to get the Cybernauts to chase us up onto the factory roof and push them through the skylight."

Emma ignored him. "And you finished it off?"

"By short-circuiting it. Water and mud into a hole in its shoulder."

"Short-circuiting . . ." Emma mused. "In the hole in the shoulder—did you see any sparking?"

Tara thought back. "Plenty of it. Like a spider's web, all over the circuitry inside."

Emma nodded as an idea came to her. "The Cybernauts are metal, Steed. They must use their metallic skin to carry electric impulses in some way. They have a sheath of plastic skin to insulate them. When the covering plastic is broken, it's possible to short-circuit the things."

"Plastic skin," Tara repeated. "That's why I wasn't electrocuted, standing in the pond."

Steed concentrated on his driving. "So what would you suggest? A long knife and a bucket of water?"

She grinned. "A bit unwieldy. How about your steel-rimmed bowler and a screwdriver?"

"Under the backseat," he replied.

Emma pulled up the seat beside her. Under it was a storage space. Inside this were a couple of bowlers and umbrellas, and a small tool kit. These were Steed's array of special weapons, all built into his everyday wear. She selected the metal-lined hat and delved into the tool chest. As she spoke, she started to work on the voice synthesizer.

"Electronic signals are a sort of language," she explained. "If you like, the commands by which an electronic brain controls a mechanical body." She tapped the voice synthesizer. "And this little gadget is designed to change language about. If I can wire it up correctly, it should be able to interfere with what passes for the thoughts of the Cybernauts and jam their circuitry. If we can scramble the commands from their brains, then the Cybernauts will have an electronic mental breakdown. I'll wire it into your hat, Steed."

"My own portable radio," Steed mused with a smile. "I wonder if it'll ever catch on—music while you walk." Then he turned serious again. "I shall be most amazed if there isn't some form of a reception committee waiting for us. This whole affair seems to have been designed to get us out to your factory. I doubt if it's just for a surprise birthday party."

Tara watched as they bantered, feeling somewhat left out of this. She was, after all, Steed's partner, yet he was discussing their plan of action with Mrs. Peel instead of her. The easy relationship that Steed had fallen back into with her bothered Tara. She knew that the two of them had been close—as close as she was with Steed?—and to watch them planning an assault while she sat by, ignorant of the science that Emma was using . . . she felt sad, inferior, and left out.

Does he want her back? she wondered. Now that Emma's husband was dead, maybe she felt free to return to the game? Or might she want Steed for other, more personal, reasons? Tara could lay claim to Steed against almost anyone else—but Mrs. Peel. How many times had she heard about the *legendary* Emma Peel from Steed himself, from

Mother, or from some other person who'd known Steed in the past? It had been bad enough when Mrs. Peel was retired—but if Emma aimed to return to action, where would that leave her?

And where would it place Steed? Tara wondered. With Emma? Or with her?

Finishing her wiring, Emma removed the bowler that Steed was wearing and placed the other on his head, carefully tilting it to precisely the angle Steed liked. He glanced at the fit in the mirror.

"What do you think, Tara?" Steed called out. "A new fashion statement?"

"I should say," Tara answered. "You're wearing it back to front. You prefer the nap running toward the collar."

"Why, so I do." He smiled at her warmly. Removing one hand from the steering wheel, he reversed the bowler. "Where would I be without you?" he asked.

He knows, Tara thought as her sinking feeling abated. He knows how I feel, and he *cares*.

"I do hope that synthesizer doesn't short out," he called over his shoulder. "Should it do so, I'll be accused of talking through my hat!"

Tara glanced at her watch. Almost one in the morning! It had been a terribly long day, but she felt little need for rest. Tonight should see the end of this case, with luck. It would be a hard fight probably, but she was confident that they would win. The only matter that she wasn't at all certain about was what would happen afterward.

Exactly thirty minutes later, the Bentley's headlights cut through the darkness as the trio pulled in to park just down the road from the Knight Industries plant. As Steed killed the motor, they all examined the blockhouse ahead of them.

"It's changed a bit since I was last here," Emma observed. "The fence is new. Still, I imagine it'll be no problem." She took a small plastic card from the waistband of her cat suit. It was a golden color. "This should get us through the electronics. My master key."

Alert for any sign of trouble, the three of them walked carefully to the front of the building. Steed scanned the street about them. Parked in one side street was a car that looked vaguely familiar; his mind refused to identify it, so he filed the information away to be checked later.

Emma paused at the gate and slipped her gold card into the waiting slot. The gate snapped open for them, and they walked through warily. Another use of the card gained them entry to the factory itself.

Unaware that they were following earlier intruders, Steed gestured toward the office door, the obvious place to start a search. Before they could reach it, the door leading to the factory opened. In the glare of light, they could see only the barest outline of four forms there. A voice spoke:

"You're rather late, I'm afraid. Still, better late than never, as they say. Will you come quietly, or would you prefer to be injured first?"

Tara recognized the voice instantly: the man who had tried to silence her and Lipp! She threw herself toward the sound, but one of the other figures moved and a metallic hand lashed out. She tried to twist, but the thing locked onto her wrist, and then stopped. Held firm by the Cybernaut, she couldn't move.

"Dear me," Cowles murmured. "What violent associates you have, Mr. Steed. Now, do you and Mrs. Peel want to try the same thing, or shall we act like civilized human beings?"

"I'm not sure about you," Steed answered cheerfully enough, "but I try to always be civilized."

Cowles didn't react to the jibe. Instead, he looked toward Tara. "How resourceful of you to escape from the house, my dear. I shall have to do better with my next attempt to kill you." He smiled at Steed and Emma, then gestured toward the remaining Cybernauts. "Allow me to reintroduce some old acquaintances."

"Time for a quick chorus of 'Auld Lang Syne'?" Steed quipped. He stepped forward, Emma following. Cowles retreated into the factory, and the Cybernaut guard dragged Tara after him. Steed, Emma, and the other two Cybernauts followed.

"It's starting to feel like a parade," Emma commented. She glanced at the metallic figures behind her and Steed. "These look like the old faithful models."

They were two of the original Cybernauts—blank-faced robots dressed in coats and hats. Their eyes were hidden behind dark glasses, and their metal hands disguised by gloves. In low light, they could move about outside and be mistaken for people. Yet these were clearly not the old generation of Cybernauts, because they moved at Cowles's vocal commands and required no form of radio control. They were clearly an improvement over Armstrong's original models.

"Déjà vu, Mrs. Peel?" asked Steed.

"Tediously familiar," Emma sighed.

"The Model-T Cybernaut," Steed joked. "Every home should have one. Who knows—one day they may replace the butler. If they can buttle."

"Enjoy your jokes now, Mr. Steed," Cowles said calmly enough. "You will shortly be too busy for that."

"Actually, I was thinking about taking a short holiday."

Cowles grinned ferociously. "Then plan on taking a *long* one—a *permanent* one. At my expense."

"How kind," Steed replied. "I must refuse, of course."

"But you have no option, Mr. Steed."

"Come now," Emma observed. "There is always an option." Then, to Steed: "They never change, do they?"

"I have often suspected," Steed replied, "that there's some poor little fellow chained to a desk somewhere—probably in the heart of the BBC—whose only task is to write trite dialogue for mad scientists. Rather like the poor folk who write those proverbs you find inside Chinese fortune cookies."

The factory was devoid of life, but the lights were all blazing. They passed work stations, bit saws, riggers, drills, and turning lathes. They passed conveyer systems, pulleys and cranes, bins full of metal turnings. Everything appeared ready for work, but there was no sign of humans anywhere—nor of more Cybernauts.

Not wishing to be left out of the conversation, Tara chipped in: "Isn't this the part where you tell us what is going on? Or is it the part where you simply gloat about how no one can stop you now?"

Cowles glared at her coldly. "I have every intention of telling you all that you wish to know. When you die, I want you to do so fully informed. It would be so crass to kill you out of hand. It will be so much more satisfying to me to watch you die in despair."

"When I die," Steed answered, "I want to do so in my bed at the age of ninety-three. Preferably with a glass of champagne in my hand."

"Dream on, Mr. Steed," Cowles told him. "You do not have ninety-three minutes left to you now."

They reached the far end of the factory, and Cowles used his own card on the door there. He turned to Emma with a smile. "You will find that even your owner's gold card won't open this lock, Mrs. Peel. So don't entertain any ideas of escape."

She smiled back. "Then I'll turn it in and ask for a refund."

It was a short walk down a narrow corridor to another room. This one was about twenty feet across, and relatively bare. A metal table stood in the middle of the room, with eight chairs about it. The chairs, Steed observed, were bolted to the floor. Two were occupied, and the occupants were handcuffed to the arms of the chairs.

"Mrs. Gale!" he exclaimed. "I trust that you are still wearing your pistol in your garter belt! And Keel, old chap! I wish I could say it was good to see you both! As it is . . ." He gestured toward the Cybernauts.

"Yes," Cathy agreed wryly. "We've already made their acquaintance."

Cowles smiled again. "Perhaps you'd be so kind

as to take a seat?" he suggested. "Of course, if you are not, then I'll simply have my Cybernauts break your legs and put you in a chair."

"Since you asked so politely," Steed replied, selecting a seat away from both Keel and Cathy. "Who's got the cards?" he asked. "We've just got time for a rubber of bridge."

"I'm not playing with you," Emma answered. "You cheat."

"Enough of this," Cowles barked, and gestured to the Cybernaut by Steed. As soon as Steed was seated, the metallic man gripped his arm, ignoring his wince of pain, and handcuffed him to the chair. Emma took a seat to his right, and Tara one to his left. Keel and Cathy were on the opposite side of the table. The Cybernauts fastened Emma and Tara, and then moved to stand impassively by the door.

"Please forgive the crudeness of the handcuffs," Cowles apologized. "But I don't wish to have to bother keeping an eye on you all as I speak. As I promised you, Miss King, I shall give you all a small, ah, briefing as to why you are here and what I aim to do with the Cybernauts."

He strode to the wall, where another of the ubiquitous slots was located. He inserted his card; the wall whined, then slid open, revealing a map of Africa with the country of Katawa highlighted. Beaming at them all, he tapped the map. "Ladies and gentlemen, I give you the beginning of the final Reich."

Tara exchanged a glance with Emma. "Another neo-Nazi nutcase," she purred.

"Hardly," Keel interrupted. "Steed, he's the brother of Klaus Drucker."

"Eisenhand," Steed murmured thoughtfully. "I thought we'd broken their grip permanently."

"He led a kind of breakaway group, I gather. They didn't approve of Eisenhand's aim to take over this country."

"Ah!" Steed smiled, beginning to understand. "They prefer a little estate in Africa instead."

"Exactly."

"He can do it, Steed," Cathy added. "The robots he has have superhuman strength. He can fashion them into the likeness of almost anyone."

"So Tara discovered. And he intends to replace the real people with their robot duplicates?" Steed completed. "He should begin with the politicians; no one would miss them."

"He's already started with M'Begwe, the Prime Minister of Katawa," Keel explained. "All he has to do is to get in to see the real M'Begwe and then kill him. The Cybernaut takes control, and the country is his."

Steed nodded. "But getting in to see the Prime Minister isn't such a simple task. M'Begwe may be popular, but he isn't foolish enough to allow potential assassins shooting room."

Cowles had been standing by patiently during this exchange, but now he beamed at Steed. "Of course not!" he agreed. "But he will trust people whom he already knows. Like Mrs. Gale," he added. He strode over to where Cathy sat and stroked her hair. She winced. "Now, Mrs. Gale he would trust . . . alone . . ." With a sudden motion, his hand moved over Cathy's face. It opened out, and there was nothing behind the façade but wiring and circuitry. Steed shuddered.

"Precisely, Mr. Steed." Cowles laughed, clearly enjoying his toying with them. He closed the face again, and it was once more Cathy looking out. "If you took my little Cybernaut for real, so will M'Begwe. Or, of course, he could see Dr. Keel." Once again he moved the faceplate aside to expose the wiring behind it. Then he closed the mask again. "Either Cybernaut is more than capable of killing him. And will do so at my command." He gestured.

Both Cybernauts simply stood up. The handcuffs holding them to the chairs snapped like icicles on a hot day. Then they marched to join their brethren at the door.

"And the real Keel and Mrs. Gale?" Steed prompted, worried for his friends.

Cowles laughed again, seeing this as weakness in Steed.

"Oh, both alive for the moment. My dear fellow, we've planned this for far too long to rush things now. When you die, you will all die together."

Emma was growing impatient. "You've tried to kill us several times already. And failed."

Shaking his head, Cowles returned to the map. "Oh, they were not serious attempts on your lives. Warm-ups, if anything. Scare tactics. Just making sure that you were in top form. I expected you to live through them. I would have been most disappointed if you had been impolite enough to die. No, they were to prepare you to face the final threat, which will certainly cause you to perish." He smiled. "But I anticipate myself.

"First of all, you must allow me to elucidate my plan of action. With the aid of my Cybernaut friends, I shall move into Katawa, of course. I have been invited there to cure their unfortunate plague. I shall naturally require a good many, ah, medical supplies. Inside the boxes will be my Cybernauts. Once I have cured the disease, I will be offered—and will accept—a high medical post in the government. Out of gratitude. Then I shall begin.

"I shall replace everyone of importance, and rule the country quietly. No one will suspect that the place is simply a stepping-stone. Katawa possesses great mineral wealth, which I will cause to be extracted. This can be used to create more Cybernauts." He tapped the map. "I shall take over each country in Africa, slowly, imperceptibly. It will look like peaceful cooperation, and I have no doubt my Cybernauts will be praised for their work. I have all the time in the world." He closed his eyes and smiled beatifically. "I have a delightful dream in which one of my Cybernauts will be awarded a Nobel Peace Prize for the work it is doing. It would be the most delectable irony, don't you think? A slow but certain takeover of African countries, which will worry no one on the international scene. And I have no need to rush things."

"I admire your patience," Steed commented. "You must be—what? Sixty? Yet you talk of all the time in the world. Your vision is interesting, but you can never live to see it come to pass."

"On the contrary!" Cowles looked triumphant, as if he'd been waiting for exactly this reply. "I am telling you the absolute truth! Why do you think the eternal Reich failed?"

"Because it was run by maniacs," Emma broke in brightly.

Cowles scowled, but refused to be baited. "Maniacs?" He laughed. "You would have to call them that, I suppose, to support your gutless, moralistic notions of life. But they were not crazy. They had vision. They saw that power is the only absolute that man can grasp for in the world. They realized that some people are fit to rule, while others are fit only to serve. Some were suited only to die. Each man and woman had their place, and will have yet again. A world of perfect order—and one that shall yet be founded; I shall see to this.

"They were men long before their time. They foresaw an eternal Reich, stretching across the world and through all the future ages. But they were only human: they tried to reach that goal in their own lifetimes. Time was against them; that could never be. Now, however, I have the solution to the two problems that caused their downfall.

"What did they lack? A true army—soldiers that would never retreat, never complain, never fall under the worst of pressures. The German people were never strong enough or dedicated enough to their tasks. They were offered their goal of immortality; their strength, their courage, their resolve failed them. But now we have the perfect soldiers for the New Reich!" He swept his hand toward the passive Cybernauts. "Look at the greatest army the world has ever known! The Cybernauts have no failings, as human troops would have. They are invincible in battle, and will face the snows of Russia or the blistering heat of the desert with equal ability. They will never falter or hesitate when they must kill!"

"And problem number two?" Steed prodded.

"What you mentioned earlier—mortality." Cowles looked at his hands, turning them over. "My hands are not as steady as they were. I've less hair, less breath, less years left to me. In the normal course of events I should have to name my successor and let him carry on my dream. Yet, as you know, dreams become diluted, or perverted, if they are passed along. My original aims might be changed, or even lost by a successor. Or worse still, I might make a wrong choice and appoint a weak, fallible leader who could bring my dreams into ashes. In the normal course of events, I should have to take those chances.

"But the normal chain of events has been broken—nay, *shattered!*—and the old mortality has gone. I shall live on to see the fruition of my dreams!"

"I think he's flipped," Emma said loudly.

"Lost his marbles," Tara agreed.

"His pilot light's gone out," Steed finished.

Cowles spun on him, eyes blazing, and struck Steed's cheek. Steed's head snapped backward, and a deep welt appeared where the fist had struck.

"Enough of your mocking!" Cowles snarled. "Be silent and listen to the last lecture of your miserable little lives." He breathed deeply until he had regained his composure, then continued. "The old Reich fell with the deaths of those who ran it. The Reich cannot live forever until the Führer himself can live forever! And now, with the aid of my knowledge and discoveries, this shall be so. I shall be the new Führer, the immortal leader of the final Reich!"

Steed coughed to regain Cowles's attention. "And how, exactly, are you immortal?"

Cowles smiled and moved closer to them. "Ah, now you listen, eh? Good, good, for I shall explain it all." He gestured at the Cybernauts once again. "These devices are the contribution of my partner, Mr. Steed. I can take no credit for the genius that made them. I am, by profession, a doctor and a geneticist. I have studied the DNA chains that are within us all—the twisted helix that describes what we all are. I have examined, and I have probed—and I can now replicate." He smiled again. "I can take one of the cells from your body and grow it within my apparatus and shape it. It will grow in a matter of months of maturity. Imagine that—from a single cell to an adult of about twenty years in a few short months!" He cocked his head to one side. "I can see that you are skeptical, Mr. Steed, but it is true. I imagine you can now see what I have done. I have taken cells from my own body and used them to make myself a new form, which lies prepared for me. When this body is too old, too infirm—then I shall take on a new one."

"And how will you do that?" asked Steed. "A brain transplant? Out with the old and in with the new?"

"Of a sort." Cowles chuckled. "You see, I have found that the memory of a person is stored in two ways. The first is electrically, like a computer, in the mind. The second is chemically, using the RNA molecules as messengers, encoded in the brain with tiny bits of information. I used my knowledge to extract and replicate these little messengers. I can then inject them into the mind of another, and thus transfer memories and information from one mind to another." He shrugged. "It doesn't work at all well on preprogrammed minds, though. I learned that during my experiments. If, shall we say, I took some of your thoughts and transferred them to Mrs. Peel's mind—"

"She'd be shocked," Tara suggested.

"Worse than that, Miss King." Cowles smiled as he recalled those experimental days. "She would go *insane*. Her mind would be torn apart by two sets of differing memories, two personalities striving for control of her body. Two sets of desires, two complete identities . . . schizophrenia of the worst possible kind." He shook himself free of the ghosts of the past. "I saw it happen too often. Both minds were thus destroyed. But if we take a fresh mind, one without thought or personality . . ."

"One that you've grown in your apparatus from your own body cells?" suggested Emma.

"I see that you understand perfectly, Mrs. Peel. I do so appreciate an intelligent audience." He glanced at the Cybernauts as he spoke. "They are wonderful inventions, but they lack true thought. Still, one mustn't complain. Yes, as you have surmised, all I have to do is to transfer my own RNA molecules to a younger version of my own body, and then I shall live on—rejuvenated, restored, and ready to take command. And when that body tires, there will be another ready for me, and another, and so on. I shall become truly immortal!"

Steed could see the horror of what Cowles had envisaged: a world ground into slavery by the Cybernauts and ruled by an immortal, insane elite. "Is this more than theory, though?" he asked.

"Oh, yes, Mr. Steed," Cowles purred. "It is much, much more than mere theory. I have succeeded in perfecting the process. I have taken the body cells and the mental RNA patterns from one individual and caused him to live again."

Suddenly chilled, Steed looked about him. "Dr. Armstrong, I presume?"

"Precisely." Cowles patted the closest of the Cybernauts, almost lovingly. "I met him a few years ago and told him some of what I envisaged. Together, we formulated the ideas that I have just expounded to you. I worked on my genetic experimentations, while he perfected his Cybernauts. As I mentioned, the memory has two portions: chemical and electrical. I worked on recording the chemical portion, he on the electrical. As you no doubt recall, he was crippled, confined to a wheelchair. I promised him a new body, with functional muscles. Then you and Mrs. Peel came along and destroyed his work—and him."

"But you nevertheless kept your promise," Emma said thoughtfully.

"Exactly. I had been prudent enough to have taken some tissue and memory samples from him during my experimental phases. And using them, I reconstructed him, grew him, and fed his memory. Dr. Armstrong has been reborn." Gesturing slightly, Cowles then admitted: "He was, of course, merely the initial experiment. I had to work faster than I had hoped, thanks to your interference. I rushed matters a trifle, and it did not turn out quite the way that I expected it to."

Steed raised an eyebrow. "So what went wrong?"

"Wrong?" a familiar voice roared. "Nothing went *wrong*, Steed!"

A doorway in the far end of the room opened, and in strode the remade Armstrong. Grinning, the apparition stood facing them. The smile on its face couldn't mask the hatred in the eyes. "But parts of me were not functional as they should have been. Parts had to be replaced with cybernetic organs. No matter: we have achieved our aim. What has happened is that I am the first of a new species—part man, part Cybernaut!"

Steed, Emma, and Tara stared in horror at what had once been Armstrong.

The body was over seven feet tall. The limbs were long, muscular, and well-built. The head was large and hairless. The right arm was metal and plastic. Pistons and wiring were its motive forces beneath the transparent plastic covering that passed for skin. Unlike the Cybernauts, Armstrong had disdained natural-looking skin. Part of his face was missing; the left eye was electronic, as was the left ear. The head from the eyes up was oversized. A metal rim gave way to more transparent plastic. Within the exposed skull lay the gray matter of a living brain. Set into this were various electronic circuits and hundreds of thin, colored wires.

With a soft hissing of hydraulics, Armstrong crossed the room toward them. "And now, Steed, class is out, and I shall have my revenge upon you all!"

16 Survival of the Fittest

"I see that the changes haven't improved your looks," Steed said.

"Or your disposition," Emma added.

"I take it he's the baddie we've all been waiting for?" Tara asked.

"More or less," agreed Steed. "Is it more or less of you in there?" he asked the apparition brightly.

Armstrong glared down at them. He raised his metal hand and the pincers snapped together. "Imagine what would happen if the next time these pincers close, they do so around one of your fingers," he suggested. "It would be sliced right off."

"It might injure my ability to write my Christmas cards." Steed looked up at him coolly. "If you were going to kill us like that, then there would have been no need for all of this production. Why go to all of this bother just to slice us up into little bits?"

Armstrong's electronic eye buzzed as it focused in on his face. "Perceptive as ever," he agreed. "But make no mistake—you and your companions have an appointment with death."

"But, first . . . ?" Steed prompted.

The cybernetic man turned and gestured toward the African map on the wall. "I see that my colleague has been explaining our plans to you. The first truly intelligent method of governing mankind! No more will they follow the whims of mere humans, subjected to their fluctuating ideas, ruled by emotions. The future of the world lies in pure logic, Steed." Armstrong tapped the glass-and-metal dome over his head. "Humans augmented with electronics, man and computer made one. The machine to compute and control the weaknesses of the flesh; the flesh to give soul and meaning to the machine." He smiled. "A sort of deus ex machina, if you like."

"I don't," Emma said. "It would work only if you can guarantee that the melding of man and machine joins the *best* of both—but in your case, I suspect the worst. Cowles speaks of a New Reich, a Führer who lives eternally. You talk of man controlled by machine. Aren't those two views somewhat incompatible?"

Cowles laughed. "Ah! The inevitable attempt to make the allies fall out, Mrs. Peel! Capital! At this point, I assume we are supposed to leap for each others' throats, allowing the three of you the opportunity to escape?"

"You can't win them all," Emma sighed.

"And you won't win this one," Armstrong promised. "Our vision is in perfect accord. Dr. Cowles and I are working to improve the human race, you see. Our work is far too important for petty bickering. We are a good team. Since my . . . rebirth, we have worked together to perfect the new generation of Cybernauts. My electronics knowledge, melded with his understanding of the human mind and body—a perfect union. He has helped me to design the features for the Cybernaut duplicates, and aided in increasing their intelligence and skill." Almost paternally, Armstrong put his arm about the Cybernaut that looked like Keel. "We have a Cybernaut whose mind is partially mechanical and partially organic. It can almost reason for itself. It took a while to produce this sophisticated form. There was one prototype that went awry—you may have heard about it, perhaps? A killer gorilla?"

"The fictional anthropoid of the news!" Steed smiled. "Yes, indeed. So that was your work?"

"Yes," Armstrong agreed. "We took something simpler than a man for our first attempt, and tried to create a perfect gorilla. It almost worked, but we lost control of it. It wandered off, and is still at large out there somewhere. It did have an advantage that we had not really foreseen, in that it lured Mrs. Gale into the action a trifle earlier than we had planned. Serendipity, you might say." The cybernetic man smiled to himself. "Cowles and I are a fine team. He has developed a form of human immortality, which I have then blended with infallibility. The result is the cybernetic man."

Steed nodded toward the hybrid. "And that," he said to Cowles, "is what you will become when you're reborn?"

"Not exactly," Cowles admitted. "As I said, I

was forced to work in the dark with Armstrong here. His death at your hands meant that I had to use older RNA for his memories, samples I had taken previously; naturally, he has no recollection of your murdering him. I was forced to accelerate the experiments, to try new techniques as I worked. Armstrong came through it well, but the problems are there to be seen. There will be improvements in the next model, of course."

"I was not able to help him design my new form," Armstrong added. "But the next time around, I shall be able to design the new cybernetics. With each rebirth, we shall become more and more perfect."

"Isn't that an oxymoron?" Tara commented. "If you're perfect now, what need for improvements?"

Armstrong glared at her. "I am not *perfect*," he agreed. "But I am *better* than a mere man."

"I don't know about that," Emma drawled. "I'd prefer a man over you any day of the week."

Ignoring her, Armstrong continued: "I still have some human failings, which must eventually be driven out."

"Such as a lust for revenge?" Steed suggested.

"Precisely."

"Well, why not start now?" Steed smiled. "You could let us go and thus gain a few Brownie points."

Despite his anger, Armstrong laughed. "Come, Steed—even you cannot be serious! No, while I have this taste for revenge, I aim to indulge it." He strode back to the table. "The three of you and your two colleagues will die—and I shall prove my superiority. The cybernetic man will triumph over all!"

Though he was trying hard to disguise it, Steed was desperately worried. Armstrong had been insane enough when he was wholly human—and this admixture of mechanical parts seemed to have sent him farther into the depths of madness. Provoking him was a dangerous game—but while they were captives like this, he and Cowles could kill them with ease. "And killing us while we're chained to chairs will prove your superiority?" he suggested.

Again Armstrong laughed. "I have no intention of killing you where you sit, Steed. Don't worry about trying to think of ways to get free—we will release you when we are ready." He snapped his pincer in front of Steed's face again. "The process of rebirth was painful for me—it was only through the addition of the cybernetic portions of my body that I could be kept alive. I accepted that. But through all the pain-filled hours of reconstructive surgery, it was merely the thought of revenge that kept me looking forward to the future. I've planned your murders in a hundred, a thousand, different ways! Oh, I had thought of simply tearing you apart while you sat here, piece by piece—" His pincer slashed out and neatly severed Steed's tie. It fell to the floor ominously. "But that would be too simple. You would have no hope. What I have planned is much, much better."

He moved away again, gesturing to the door that led back to the factory. "You will all be set free out there. Then I shall pursue and fight you all to the death. That will be much more satisfying, because you will have the illusion of a chance. You will delude yourself into thinking that you *might* just beat me. Then, when I do finally kill you all, your despair will be that much more satisfying to me."

"And what if we do beat you?" Steed asked.

Armstrong looked at him and then burst into laughter. "What an absurd thought!" Abruptly he stopped laughing and sneered. "You don't stand a chance, Steed. Not a hope in hell. But keep on thinking it. It will make my victory so much sweeter."

"And that," Emma commented to Steed, "is supposed to be better than human?"

"Maybe he's got his circuits crossed?" Steed suggested.

"Joke all that you wish," Armstrong said. "It will not help you."

"We haven't done so badly so far," Tara replied. "Every time you've made us targets, we've survived."

"My dear girl," Cowles said, smiling, "as I have already explained, those previous attempts were not meant to kill you. They were—shall we say—appetizers? To help us to savor that final moment. To prepare you for this moment, to lead you here."

"Then why frame Steed and Mother?"

"Purely for the fun of it," Cowles admitted. "The thought of setting the Department at each other's throats was exquisite. To engender suspicion and distrust, to set Steed and Mother against one another. It distracted everyone from our major plotting, and allowed us the opportunity to plant all of the clues that we had constructed to lead you here."

Armstrong nodded. "Cowles thought of it. He had his own reasons to hate you and Keel, Steed.

And I to seek revenge on you and Mrs. Peel. We added both Mrs. Gale and Miss King to make the collection complete. We are not content with a simple vendetta. We will obliterate you all, and all that you work with and stand for."

"Hence the takeover of this plant," Cowles added. "We did need a base of operations, and it seemed to us to be particularly appropriate that Mrs. Peel should inadvertently contribute to the success of our endeavors."

"And after we are . . . disposed of?" Steed prompted.

"Then we shall use our Cybernauts to destroy Mother and to throw the Department into utter chaos," Cowles explained. "We have a delightful replica of Miss King ready to send out to do the job. There will be a witch hunt inside British Intelligence that will divert all attention from us."

"Then we sail to Katawa," Armstrong elaborated. "The Cybernauts of Mrs. Gale and Dr. Keel will assassinate the real Prime Minister M'Begwe, and we shall substitute our own. Then we shall work slowly toward the unification of the world—one government, one destiny, one cybernetic mind!"

Emma smiled sweetly at Cowles. "And what do *you* want to be when you grow up?"

"Enough of this," Cowles sighed. "You abuse our patience. I think the time has come for you to meet Keel and Gale. Then—blitzkrieg."

"I agree." Armstrong nodded. His mechanical-human body moved toward them. His pincer reached out toward Tara's wrist. Unable to stop herself, she cringed back. Armstrong laughed as his pincer snapped shut—

—neatly severing the handcuffs that held her to the chair. Still laughing, he performed the same feat on Emma and Steed. Then he stood back and gestured toward the door.

"Out there," he snapped. "Feel free to roam about. I shall come after you in exactly ten minutes."

"Be prompt," Steed urged. "I abhor tardiness." He touched the brim of his hat lightly, then moved to the door. He held it open for his companions and closed it behind him.

His practiced calm fled the moment the door was closed. Emma could see the uncertainty and fear in his eyes.

"What are our chances of winning?" she asked.

"Practically nonexistent," Steed admitted. "The advantage lies with Armstrong. His new body may be half machine, but I suspect he is much faster than he wishes us to believe."

"Then we must level the odds," Tara snapped. "We *have* to beat him."

They emerged from the corridor into the factory. To get out there, they passed two immobile-looking Cybernauts. In the center of the floor were Keel and Cathy.

"My dear Mrs. Gale!" Steed called out cheerfully. "And Keel, old man! It's good to see you both."

"You've picked a strange place for a reunion," Cathy said dryly. She eyed both Emma and Tara.

So did Keel. He grinned. "I see that you've

hitched up with *two* new dolly birds, Steed," Keel joked.

Emma glared back at him. "Colleagues," she corrected.

"Partners," Tara added.

"Friends," Steed finished.

Cathy grunted playfully. "Don't tell me that you've finally accepted the equality of the sexes?"

"I have become enlightened." Steed smiled. "These young ladies can be most persuasive." As he talked, he looked around the factory floor. "There's plenty of possibilities here," he commented to Emma. "Drills, lathes, chisels . . ."

Emma nodded and checked the closest of the presses. The power was dead. She grimaced and glanced at the far wall. The fuses and circuit breakers were in clear sight—right by the two Cybernauts. "Nothing ventured . . ." She ambled casually across the room. Equally casually, the Cybernauts came to life, moving to protect the panels. Raising an eyebrow, Emma sauntered back. "I think that idea has been overruled."

Tara had discovered a hand drill on one bench, and set it spinning. "This works."

"And so does this," Cathy replied, spinning a vise at another machine. "David and I haven't been wasting our time, either."

Keel scowled in thought. "Let's be ridiculously optimistic for a minute," he said, "and assume that we can all somehow defeat this Armstrong fellow. What about the small army of Cybernauts that Cowles still has? You've faced them before, Steed—do they have any weaknesses?"

"In the past, yes," Steed replied. "They needed

external commands. But this is a new generation of Cybernauts. They seem to have more computerized minds." He nodded toward the two on guard. "You saw how they anticipated Mrs. Peel's moves without being ordered into place."

"It doesn't look too good for us," muttered Keel.

"I don't know how it was in your days," Tara commented, "but Steed and I have gotten out of worse spots than this. I just wish I could remember what they were."

The door at the far end opened again. Cowles strode in with four more of his Cybernauts. Smiling in anticipation, he moved to one side.

Armstrong had to bend to get through the doorway. The bright lights gleamed off his polished metal and plastic. With a feral smile, he moved out into the room.

"Time to die . . ." he breathed.

17 Apocalypse Now . . . and Again

Without a word, Steed and his companions spread out among the maze of dead machinery. Armstrong watched, apparently in no hurry to slake his thirst for revenge. He seemed amused by their lack of coordinated effort. Slowly he moved forward, and his five opponents backed away.

"Come," he called. "No heroes? No one willing to risk all to buy time for their friends? You disappoint me."

Tara moved first, dashing toward him, her long legs eating up the ground. Armstrong laughed in delight and reached out his human arm as if to embrace her. But she wasn't foolish enough to get within his grasp. Instead, she jumped to the side, onto the flat bed of a drill press and used that to leap over Armstrong's head, her arms reaching for and gripping a light fixture. Using her momentum, she swung around and slammed her legs hard into his back.

The cybernetic creature staggered under the blow but didn't fall. Instead, he shook himself and twisted, to try to grab Tara. She dropped to the ground and sprinted away as fast as she had attacked. Furious at his failure to catch her, Armstrong snatched at the drill instead. Exerting his strength, he wrenched at the machine until the head of it snapped free of the restraining bolts. The jagged metal had to weigh a good two hundred pounds, but he hefted it and then threw it like a harpoon toward Tara's back.

Cathy dived across the floor, neatly slicing Tara's legs from under her with a roundhouse kick. Both women fell in a tangle as the machinery whipped over their heads and embedded itself in the wall with a thundering crash. Tara nodded her thanks as she and Cathy dived for further cover.

Steed moved in, discarding the covering of his umbrella. The handle was now attached to a wicked-looking sword. He moved in toward Armstrong, brandishing the sword menacingly. The hybrid man reached out with his metal arm and sliced off most of Steed's blade with a pincerlike claw.

Before Steed could react to the loss, Armstrong backhanded him—with the human arm, luckily. Steed slammed backward, colliding with a workbench. The pain in his chest from the blow was matched by the agony in his back. His vision danced, yellow-hazed, and his ears rang. He knew that he was a perfect target for Armstrong now. He couldn't summon up the energy to focus, much less to move out of the way.

Seeing Armstrong moving in for the kill, Emma grabbed for a length of the chain that fed the overhead crane. She swung herself over the top of a drill and down directly in Armstrong's path, blocking his access to Steed. The cybernetic man laughed and continued his relentless advance as Emma dropped into a crouch, knowing how useless this would be.

Before Armstrong reached her, there was movement behind him. Keel had found a large waste dumper and wheeled it into place. Kicking off from one piece of machinery, he threw everything he had behind the rolling trolley. It caught Armstrong by surprise, neatly slicing his legs out from under him. With a cry of shock, he collapsed in a tangle with the cart. Keel followed through, aiming a hard kick at the glass-and-steel skull.

His foot jarred with pain as he connected. Hobbling back, he stared in horror as Armstrong rolled over. The waste cart didn't pin him down at all. Instead, he tore it apart with the pincer arm, then started throwing the jagged bits of metal around. Keel dived for cover as one piece whanged off the machinery by his head. A second narrowly missed Emma as she dodged aside.

The action had bought Steed the time he needed to clear his head. Clutching his ribs, which felt as though they were on fire, he crawled aside. He saw his bowler lying where it had fallen; he grabbed it and set it back on his head. The weight of it reminded him of the voice synthesizer there.

He remembered the flashing circuitry that he

had seen in the exposed portion of Armstrong's brain, and the metallic mounting plate in the skull. Inspiration struck him, but he knew he'd never be able to carry off his plan alone. He needed help . . .

Armstrong had finished shredding and throwing the pieces of the cart. Glaring angrily now, he looked about for a human victim to vent his rage on. He saw Keel crouched behind one of the lathes and stormed over toward it. Keel looked startled and tried to retreat. Armstrong thrust his cybernetic arm through the gap in the machinery and grabbed Keel's arm. Slowly, he closed the pincer, watching the pain grow in Keel's face. He didn't see Cathy until it was too late.

She slapped the restraining bolts on the armature of the lathe and then slammed it forward on its rollers. It caught Armstrong's metal limb with a sickening crunch. The pincer opened and Keel fell free, groaning. The impact had not hurt Armstrong physically, but the force of the blow had dented the metal arm, and part of the plastic "skin" had cracked. With a roar of rage, he jerked his arm free and hurled the armature backward with such force that it snapped clean off the rails.

Cathy dived aside as this projectile bore down on her, but she wasn't quite quick enough. Pain lanced through her back as the metal sliced cloth and skin. The force of the blow rolled her to one side: the missile smacked loudly but harmlessly into another of the machines before slamming to the floor. As Cathy dragged herself to her feet, she could feel the blood oozing out of the shattered skin on her shoulders. Risking a quick glance to ascertain Armstrong's position, she moved away from him as quickly as she could. Every step was agony.

Then Keel was by her, holding her up and leading her away. Armstrong, victorious again, laughed with pleasure and started after them.

Steed had finally caught Emma's attention, and she hesitated for a moment—go to Steed, or help Cathy? Steed saw her indecision and beckoned even more furiously. Reluctantly, she joined him. He handed her his bowler, which she stared at uncomprehendingly.

"The signal generator," he hissed, so his voice wouldn't carry. "We aimed to try it on a Cybernaut—so how about their big brother? That metal plate in his head should conduct your signals."

"I'm not sure, Steed. I set it thinking I'd be using it to scramble a mechanical brain," she protested.

"A good part of his now is mechanical. I'd gamble that the parts keeping the cybernetics working also keep him alive."

"You'd gamble what?" she countered.

"Our lives," he said, getting to his feet. "See what you can do."

Ignoring her pull on his trouser leg, Steed set off down the gangway toward Armstrong. The huge man/machine had almost reached Cathy and Keel when Tara dashed out of hiding, slamming into him with all her force.

It was pointless, really. He was so much more massive than she that she simply bounced back. Armstrong laughed again and grabbed at her with his human hand. It closed about Tara's neck, and he started to squeeze.

Steed wrenched free a length of piping, half shattered by flying debris from the battle. Swinging it over his head, he slammed it down hard onto Armstrong's arm.

For the first time, the cybernetic man gave a scream of sheer pain. His human half was tough, but the pipe was tougher, designed as it had been to hold fluids under pressure. It left a large, bleeding welt in the forearm, and Armstrong let Tara fall to the floor, where she lay gasping for her breath. Screaming wordlessly, Armstrong turned on Steed.

Weakened by the previous blows, Steed reacted too slowly. The metal pincer lashed out, fastening about his throat. Armstrong dragged him closer, cutting off his breath. Human and mechanical eyes stared gloatingly into Steed's fogging human ones.

"Good-bye, Steed," he hissed. "You've put up a good fight. But I expected no less." He started to slowly close the claw about Steed's neck.

"Steed!"

As his vision wavered, Steed heard Emma cry out. She threw his bowler over the room, spinning it accurately toward him. His fingers clutched for it, but the metal brim of the hat smacked against the outside of his hand and fell to the floor. Heedless, Armstrong stepped back, his mechanical foot coming down to crush the bowler.

Tara, still fighting to recover her breath, wrenched the hat out of Armstrong's way a second before it would have been pulverized. Hearing the hum from it, she realized what Steed and Emma were trying to do. If she only had the strength to get up and finish the job . . .

Keel couldn't understand what the significance of the bowler was, but if Tara had risked her fingers to recover it, then it had to be of more than sartorial importance. He left Cathy propped against a lathe and scurried to Tara's side. As he took the hat from her, she managed to choke out: "Head . . ."

At first he couldn't comprehend her anxiety, but Tara made a pulling motion toward her head, then gestured at the hybrid killer. He got the picture: the bowler was for Armstrong's head. He dashed in, ducking a reflexive blow from the cybernetic man, and then slammed the hat down hard on Armstrong's skull.

The pincers halted their convulsive grip on Steed's throat and let him fall in a heap on the floor. Armstrong stiffened, his human eye glazing over in sudden fear. He tried to raise his mechanical arm to brush the hat from his head, but it refused to obey his mental commands. Sweat broke out on him as he struggled to retain command of his mechanical parts. Then he tried to raise his human hand, but Steed's blow had damaged him badly. His hand was a mass of pain and he couldn't reach up with it.

Through what was visible of the glass dome of his skull, the flashing circuits in his brain were beginning to overheat from the conflicting activity. Keel could see the results of his actions. The random signals being generated by the sound synthesizer were blocking off his thoughts and switching off the cybernetic connectors that loaded Armstrong's cybernetic portions of brain tissue.

With a gasp, the creature lurched as his leg seized into place. The fail-safes locked it into position as circuit after circuit failed. With mounting panic, he realized that the mechanical parts of his body were failing one after another, which meant that—

Armstrong gave a terrible, howling scream as his mechanical heart stopped functioning. In this one last, lingering sound, his body collapsed forward. Supported by the locked leg, it slumped over. The bowler finally fell from his head, smoking, revealing the cracked and molten cover to the braincase. Liquefied glass mixed with gray matter, trickling down the shattered skull.

Cowles finally woke to the fact that something had gone terribly wrong. He had been enjoying watching Armstrong fight. Steed and his friends had battled well, providing good entertainment. In fact, Cowles wasn't too worried about who would win the fight. Armstrong had yet to prove whether his cybernetic body was as good as he claimed. If it was, he would be a worthy ally; if not, then he would not be missed. In either eventuality, Cowles had his own plans to ensure that none of the victims survived to stop him.

As Armstrong died, Cowles screamed: "Fool! Idiot! Unstoppable, he told me! Impervious to pain!" But so it went: he could never rely on a human ally, but he still had Armstrong's best and most valuable addition to his plans.

"Kill them all," he ordered the Cybernauts beside him.

The impassive robotic creations started to move out. Each of the Cybernauts moved independently, selecting its victim. Cowles smiled happily. Exhausted from their fight with Armstrong, Steed and his friends would never survive this assault. . . .

Steed finally managed to take a deep breath. He staggered to his feet and recovered his smoking bowler. It was completely unwearable now, but it still had its uses.

As the first Cybernaut moved in, Steed forced his aching body into one last move. He threw his bowler with all his might. Spinning somewhat erratically, the steel-rimmed hat smashed into the face of the robot. The plastic skin snapped and the metal brim sank into the circuitry beneath. In a shower of sparks and flames, the Cybernaut collapsed backward.

As the Cybernaut that had targeted her closed in, Emma feinted forward, then ducked under the responding blow. It whistled harmlessly over her head and she sprang up, pushing the arm farther around on its trajectory, into the side of one of the machines. A drill, she noted. Hitting the release on the drill, she slapped over the lever controlling its vertical descent. Though it wasn't spinning, the drill still slammed down on the Cybernaut's arm with enough force to penetrate the metal and plastic and to pin the arm to the base of the machine.

The robotic creature struggled, trying to drag its arm free. With a gleeful smile, Emma grabbed up a sheet of metal debris from the floor and smashed in the faceplate of the Cybernaut. It collapsed forward, twitching.

Tara had regained her feet by the time her attacker reached her. It punched out: she ducked the blow and danced aside. The second blow also missed her as she staggered away from the creature, still trying to regain her energy. Ahead of her was another of the rubbish carts, and she moved around behind it. The Cybernaut was about ten feet away. Bracing herself against a lathe, she kicked out at the cart with both feet.

It rolled right at the Cybernaut, which belatedly tried to move aside. The cart slammed into it, knocking it backward into another lathe. The impact smashed parts of the robot: it collapsed into a sparking pile of metal and flames.

Cathy could not regain her feet; the pain in her back was still excruciating. As the Cybernaut lumbered toward her, she cast about for inspiration. The length of piping Steed had hit Armstrong with lay within reach, and she reeled it in. As the Cybernaut lunged for her, she rammed upward with all of her might behind the pipe. She had noted the weakness of the faces of the Cybernauts, and aimed the blow right between the eyes . . .

The robot staggered backward, clawing helplessly at the metal spear. Flailing about, it fell over, and then was still.

The last two Cybernauts were the ones that looked like Keel and Cathy. This pair had targeted Keel, who was not prepared to wait around for them. He dived to one side and dodged between two drills. They were unable to move as quickly as he was, and he gained a few yards on them. He ran toward Cowles, who was still reeling from the shock of seeing his supposedly invincible Cybernauts being systematically demolished. Belatedly he realized the danger he was in, and his hand went to his pocket, dragging out a small control unit. He had naively assumed that his Cybernauts were more than enough force to deal with Steed and his companions. It was time to call in reinforcements.

Keel hit him low and dirty, before he could do so. Cowles squealed and gasped, doubling over from the blow. As the two Cybernauts closed in, Keel whipped Cowles around into their path, using him as a shield.

Two metal arms snapped out, each delivering a lethal karate blow. Instead of hitting Keel, however, both slammed into Cowles. His body went limp, and Keel let it fall. The two Cybernauts hesitated, and Keel scooped up Cowles's hand-sized control unit. Not having the slightest idea which button turned the Cybernauts off, Keel simply spun about and smashed it against the closest piece of machinery. With a satisfying grinding and breaking of components, the unit fell to pieces. Keel dropped the wreckage and turned back to the Cybernauts. Both of the cybernetic creatures had ground to a halt, frozen in mid-stride.

In the sudden silence as Keel glanced around, he realized he was shaking.

The factory looked like Armageddon had been fought there. Cybernaut bodies smoked and sparked. Shattered machinery leaked oil. Armstrong's corpse was still bent over, supported grotesquely by his mechanical leg. The four other survivors picked themselves up slowly, looking about at the devastation.

Emma brushed her hair back from her eyes. "I think this place could do with a refit," she finally managed.

"So could I," sighed Tara, grimacing as she massaged her right arm. She looked in concern at Steed, who still had a bright red welt about his neck from the pincer grip. "How are you feeling?"

"Like a goldfish run over by a tank," he confessed. He touched his neck and decided against repeating that move for quite a while. His throat felt as if it had been cut.

Cathy tried to get to her feet. Concerned, Keel moved to her side and helped her. She rewarded him with a smile that held more than a hint of the pain that she felt. "I hope you're a very good doctor," she grunted. "Because I need one right now."

"He's the best," Steed told her with a hint of his old smile. "I only work with the best. All of you," he added, looking them over.

Cocking her head to one side, Emma laughed softly. "Steed," she murmured, "you're turning into an old flatterer."

"Not *that* old," he replied. He looked around at the mess. "I hope you don't want us to clean the place up."

"Certainly not," Emma replied, taking his arm. "To the victors, the spoils."

"Meaning?" Tara asked, deliberately taking Steed's other arm in a very possessive fashion.

"Meaning," Emma amplified, "that I have learned something from my years of association with Steed. One of my executive orders to every factory I own is concerning beverages. Even as we speak, unless I am very much mistaken, there should be a bottle of Krug champagne in the office, chilling to perfection."

"Bless you, Mrs. Peel," said Steed. "Lead the way!"

Cathy joined Keel and looked appraisingly at her Cybernaut counterpart. "Does that really look like me?" she asked.

"No more than the other resembles me," he assured her. He took one last look at his double. "I can't help feeling like I've killed myself."

"Strangest suicide I've ever seen," murmured Cathy, and Keel chuckled. As he helped her to pick her way through the debris, he caught her amused glance at the trio in front of them. He knew his eyes mirrored her amusement. "Trust Steed," he growled. "Not only does he win the battle, but he gets two pretty girls to fight over him."

"Jealous?" Cathy asked.

"No," he answered cheerfully. "After all, I'm remembering that you and I are still due to fly out to Katawa and spend several months there. We'll be out in the hills without a chaperone." He tightened his grip on her. "And I'm looking forward to it immensely."

Cathy looked him over appraisingly. "So am I," she finally admitted. "So am I."

EPILOGUE

Mother levered himself into position in the howdah with a sigh of deep satisfaction. It was very ornate, with delicate gilded scrollwork over the boxlike body. The canopy overhead was of red velvet, with blue tassles. Rhonda took up her usual station by his side. Steed clambered in behind him, patting his bowler into place.

"Everything's worked out fine," Mother told him. "Charles and I had a long chat with the Minister and showed him what was left of that voice synthesizer. There's a good chance we'll get that Lipp chappie to build us another model when he gets out of the hospital. Had sensitive ears apparently, and got tinnitus from all that noise."

"Ah," said Steed, hating to be the bearer of ill tidings. "I'm afraid you're too late there. Mrs. Peel has already had the professor sign a contract. Seems that Knight Industries is very interested in funding further research for him. And Mrs. Gale has a notion that she may be able to use it in an attempt to communicate with her gorillas. She tells me that their vocal cords can't shape words properly, but that with Lipp's device . . ."

"Ah, well." Mother sighed theatrically. "I doubt that Lipp would have been amenable to signing the Official Secrets Act, anyway."

"I take it that you and I are fully exonerated?" Steed asked.

"Fully," Mother informed him. "There's even a commendation for you out of all this. But there's still a few loose ends, you know. Did you ever find where Cowles had done his laboratory work?"

"No," Steed admitted. "He had mentioned growing himself a new body, but we found no traces of one."

"So," Mother concluded glumly, "we can't be certain that he'll stay dead, then?"

Steed shrugged. "I don't think there's too much to worry about there. He'd never have trusted anyone else with the secrets of how to wake that other body—they might have used it for their own memories instead."

"Well, let's hope you're right." Mother held out a hand and Rhonda passed him the rocket launcher that Steed had used. "This looks awfully familiar. Had a report that one was missing from Wendworth Downs, you know."

"Really? Some people will take anything that isn't tied down," Steed replied, adjusting his bowler to a lower angle.

"Quite," Mother agreed. He accepted one of the missiles from Rhonda's grip and loaded the launcher. "And how about Mrs. Peel? Gone back to work again now?"

Steed looked thoughtful. "I believe so. She didn't seem too happy about the whole thing, though."

Mother's eyes twinkled. "Think she might be amenable to being reactivated, eh?"

"Perhaps."

Mother nodded. "I'll give it some thought and speak with the Minister about it. She was always one of the best. You have good judgment, Steed."

"I've had some excellent help over the years. Dr. Keel, Mrs. Gale . . ."

"How are they doing?" Mother asked, nodding to Rhonda. "I heard they're both now in Katawa."

"They've hit it off famously." Steed smiled. "Like long-lost friends. No longer ships that pass in the night—they've found a mutual port in a storm, I suspect. And we did find Cowles's notes on his artificial plague virus, which will help in bringing the problems in Katawa under firm control."

"First class, absolutely first class," Mother concluded. "So all that's left is this rampaging mechanical gorilla, then?"

"Right," Steed agreed.

"Then let's bag it," said Mother, placing the rocket launcher on his knees.

Rhonda nodded to the mahout, who was perched on the neck of the elephant. He dug in with his knees, and his massive charge slowly rose from where it had been sitting. The howdah wavered slightly, then settled in place as the elephant started to amble off. Ahead of them, beaters worked at the woods.

Steed held onto his bowler, enjoying the rolling gait as the elephant marched along. Still, maybe he should have sent Tara in to report instead. "I love your new transport."

"Splendid, isn't it? Borrowed it from a friend in the circus," Mother informed him. "Between that and this"—he hefted the rocket launcher—"we should be able to finish off that gorilla thingy. Which reminds me, Steed. Did I ever tell you about the time I stalked a killer tiger in my days with the raj in India? Well . . ."